# TROUBLE IN
# TIONESTA

## HOW THE WORLD SHOULD END

ROBERT PRINGLE

Order this book online at www.trafford.com
or email orders@trafford.com

Most Trafford titles are also available at major online book retailers.

Printed in the United States of America.

ISBN: 978-1-4907-3114-8 (sc)
ISBN: 978-1-4907-3116-2 (hc)
ISBN: 978-1-4907-3115-5 (e)

Library of Congress Control Number: 2014905101

Because of the dynamic nature of the Internet, any web addresses or links contained in
this book may have changed since publication and may no longer be valid. The views
expressed in this work are solely those of the author and do not necessarily reflect the
views of the publisher, and the publisher hereby disclaims any responsibility for them.

Any people depicted in stock imagery provided by Thinkstock are models,
and such images are being used for illustrative purposes only.
Certain stock imagery © Thinkstock.

*Trafford rev. 03/20/2014*

www.trafford.com
North America & international
toll-free: 1 888 232 4444 (USA & Canada)
fax: 812 355 4082

For my mother and father
May they rest in peace

# CHAPTER ONE

I t all started off innocently enough with a small lump of ice in the asteroid belt getting a slight nudge from a piece of soviet space junk that was launched in 1959. The lump traveled a short distance and collided with a much larger object that headed out into the solar system towards the sun. Sorta like a small misjudgment on the pool table where the eight ball falls in by accident.

As it neared Mars it was picked up by an observer in Peru who noticed the odd blue color. He posted his finding on the internet but had the bad luck of a nova erupting in the Scorpio Constellation that everyone else focused on including him at the same time. It went unnoticed.

What no one knew was the mineral composition of the half mile wide object. It approached the sun and was pulled into the firey maelstrom and exploded, producing gamma rays that were emitted towards earth. It also caused a chain reaction in the solar mass.

As the gamma rays approached Earth they reacted with the radiation in the Van Allen belt, changing them in some inexplicable way. They raced through the atmosphere and struck the Earth.

Fifty miles from Bejing, Ho Lin approached his chicken pen. His only child, a daughter, was to be wed this day. He had spent all his savings on her dress and had to provide the wedding feast. He knew that he and his wife would go hungry without the eggs in the future but he was only concerned of saving face by his new in-laws. He slaughtered all six of his hens and the rooster. The birds had been exposed to avian bird flu two years prior but had shown no ill effects.

If his daughter's wedding would have been held one day later he would have noticed the sickness. The unforeseen gamma rays affected the virus in the birds causing it to mutate. A mote of dust got in his eye and he rubbed it with his blood stained hands. He finished cleaning the chickens and brought them in to his wife to prepare. After washing up he picked up his good luck stick and rubbed it between his hands. His joss had been good to wed his daughter to such a wealthy and well connected family, perhaps it would continue to smile on him.

Rusty Griffen hoisted the air powered gun and pulled the trigger. With the force of a twelve gauge shotgun it drove a steel ball into the cows forehead. The cow collapsed and was pushed onto the conveyer where it would enter the slaughter house of the meat packing firm he worked at in Kansas. The steel ball was attached to a spring which retracted back into the barrel to be ready for the next beeve.

Three cows down the line was an old heifer that had been found wandering on the open land about a mile from the new CDC facility just relocated from Plum Island, New York. Joe Bissel didn't ask any questions, he removed the metal tag from the cow's ear and tossed it on the ground. He blessed his luck as he could sell the cow to old Sim at the slaughterhouse with no questions asked, he didn't like questions. He really needed new tires on his old pickup and here God provided the means.

What he didn't know was that the cow had been infected with mad cow virus. It slipped out of its holding pen when a new hire at the research lab was busy doing a couple lines of meth and forgot about shutting the gate. He had been clean when he took the mandatory drug test the week before and figured they wouldn't be testing him right away. Later, he miscounted the cows.

The gamma rays hit the animal at first light and once again mutated a virus. When Rusty's shift was over he stopped off in final cuts and got a nice slice of sirloin for his dinner. Rusty liked his steak rare, really rare. Ten seconds a side on the grill outside his mobile home and half a bottle of A1 and he was chewing away.

He washed it down with his first bud light and lit a Marlboro. Went inside and turned on his TV, there was a new episode of Duck Dynasty on and he sat back on his old recliner, he belched and popped open another brewski.

# CHAPTER TWO

Arnold Swende was having a good day, his wife Mattie had been particularly frisky last night. His boy Clay, went off to school without a fuss and he learned at work a new contract came through guaranteeing two more years of steady employment. That took away a lot of stress, things had been iffy there for awhile.

Arnie was thirty three and still in reasonable health, the hair wasn't thinning like most of his old classmates and he kept the bills paid. He was changing one of the bits on the cnc router he ran at Precision Parts of Titusville when his boss wanted to talk to him.

"Arnie, I got a question for ya." Big Mike the supervisor said.

"Shoot away." Arnie answered.

"Well, you ever think about running the internal lathe?" Mike looked at him with his eyebrows raised. "Sam is going to retire next month and he said he wanted you to take it over."

"The lathe? Shit yeah Mike, I'm getting bored with this old girl," Arnie replied waving his hand at his machine.

"Okay, now here's how it works. Monday, you start training this new fella we hired. One week should do it, I already checked him out and he has real experience. Then you go over to Sam for three weeks." Mike leaned against the wall. "Oh, by the way that job pays a buck and a half more an hour, how's that suit you?" Mike asked with a big shit eating grin on his rugged face.

"Holy shit Mike, that suits me just fine, yes sir, just fine." Arnie nodded at him with his mouth open and a smile creeping in.

"Good, now be sure and thank Sam at lunch now, ya hear?" Mike gave him an atta boy pat on the back then turned and walked off towards his office.

"Yeah, yeah sure, holy shit." Arnie stood there for a minute then said, "son of a bitch," to no one at all.

Mattie was putting the wet clothes in the dryer right about then, thinking about their love making the night before. We got a good high score on that one she thought and giggled to herself.

At thirty two she still looked good and having the baby seven years back hadn't ruined her figure at all. They got along well with only an occasional spat now and again. She was laid off from the cabinet shop where she had worked in assembly, but she was starting to like the stay at home mom thing.

Clay was such a sweet child she sometimes wondered if all that was for real. She reached down and rubbed Goofy behind his ears. He was a mixed mutt that they found sleeping on their back porch. Clay had begged so hard to keep him they just couldn't say no. He was smart and housebroken and really loved Clay.

"You are a goofy mutt, aren't you?" She said as she scratched his head. He wagged his tail, agreeing wholeheartedly. "Well kiddo, it's time to test the waters." She said and went up to the bathroom. She got the home pregnancy test down from where she hid it and got it ready. The darn thing was expensive she thought, but cheaper than a doctor. "Tinkle, Tinkle, little star, how we wonder why we are." She recited, Her mother taught her that to make potty training fun. I wonder if the mutt thinks I'm crazy, she mused looking at Goofy who was watching her with his head cocked and his ears arched. She put the kit in the sink and waited. She caught her breath as the line appeared and changed her life.

Math sucks, thought Clay as he added up the numbers. They had to put away their laptops and do this exercise the lotech way with pencil and paper. It was sooo much easier using the calculator built into the portable computer they had been issued at the start of second grade. It was now mid October and not many nice days left. He looked up in time to catch Sally Pinker smiling at him. He smiled back, Sally was okay for a girl but why was she always smiling at him?

"Okay Class, pass your papers up to the front. Be sure your name is on the top of the page." Mrs. Reddick the second grade teacher said. "It's almost time for lunch, so clear those desks. When we return from recess we will take a look at trees and how they grow." Then the lunch bell rang.

# CHAPTER THREE

Bob Prince paid for his dinner at the Cashiers station, picked up his clothes bag and headed out of the truck stop towards the parking lot. At fifty four he knew his driving days were numbered. H e was battling high blood pressure and was now having trouble seeing at night. If he sat in the seat longer than four hours at a time his back ached. Thirty two years of the long haul wears hard on a man.

"Hey mister, you a truck driver?" a ladies voice asked. He turned to see a young woman in a baggy windbreaker and jeans.

"Yes I am and no I'm not." Bob replied as he started walking again.

"What do you mean you are and you're not?" she asked back.

"Yes I'm a trucker and no, I'm not looking for a fifteen minute date." Bob stated matter of factly.

"Well, I'm no damned whore but I do need a ride." She spoke a little testily.

"Really, Then you should have asked which direction I was going instead." Bob came right back at her. "I'm headed east and I'm in a hurry so quit bothering me."

"Wait, is New York east? I don't know directions all that well." The woman said.

Bob looked at her. She could do with some cleaning up but she stood steady and her eyes were clear. "I know better but you got any gear? If I don't like you I'll drop you at the next exit."

"Oh, okay, wait, its right over there, don't leave, please." She spun around and ran to the hedge outside the Sapp Brothers outside

Omaha, grabbed a small backpack like a kid would have for school and ran back. "This is it, all I have." She panted.

"Well, let's go, I don't get paid to stay in one spot." With that Bob turned and started for his truck.

"I'm Sadie, Sadie Sullivan." She said.

"Bob." He answered a little roughly. "There's the truck." It was his truck, Bob was a member of a fast disappearing breed, the owner/ operator. The truck was a thirty year old Western Star, the Cadillac of semis. With its long nose and double wide sleeper, custom chrome, and chicken lights it was a trucker's truck. Bob paid twenty thousand for it used. He had rebuilt the motor three times, the transmission six, replaced both rear drives and just about every service part on it. He knew everything about that truck and would never get rid of it.

"You mind where you put your feet, don't even touch the paint." He said as he unlocked the passenger door. The interior was done in brown leather down in Mexico, thick plush dark brown carpet, it was the cleanest vehicle Sadie had ever seen. Both seats were custom captains that seemed to fold around you when you sat in them. Its name was Maggie.

The exterior was deep brown, polished and waxed. Polished aluminum oversized fuel tanks and the wheels were polished aluminum also. Bob owned the trailer too, a forty eight footer painted a matching brown with a forty mule team rig custom painted on each side. Bob liked his truck. With a twelve cylinder Cat motor and eighteen speed transmission it would eat up some miles and waste no time doing it. It held four hundred gallons of fuel.

He fired it up and let it idle for a little while. "I used to never shut it off but with all the damn taxes on fuel now I'm barely making any money." He put it in gear and let up on the clutch easing it on up to the truck stops exit.

"Hey there Caretaker, where you headed?" the cb radio squawked.

"Headed to the dirty side, who's this?" Bob replied.

"You got the number one Sidewinder here going to the Gay Bay."

"I hear that. Catch you on the flip, I gotta rooooll amigooo." And Bob did roll down the on ramp of I-80 and was doing sixty five at the bottom. Sadie was staring at Bob with her mouth open. "What the . . ." she started to say. "Look here Missy, rule number one, no shoes in the truck. Take them off and put them in this bag." He said as he handed her a plastic bag.

Sadie took the bag and slipped her sneakers off without a word. Two minutes later, "Sweet desperate Jesus, put 'em back on, put 'em back on. Maam, I gotta ask, when was the last time you had a bath?"

"It's none of your damn business, you son of a bitch, let me off at the next place." Sadie began to cry.

. "All right now stop that crying, damn it, there's no crying in trucking until you look at your paycheck." Bob was getting concerned. "Look why don't you tell me how you ended up in a godforsaken place like Sapp Brothers? Wait, when did you eat last, are you hungry? Do you have clean clothes if I got you a shower? Come on now, answer me true."

"I am hungry." She said and started to cry again. Bob crossed over into Iowa and stopped at the next truck stop.

"Come on, let's get some food in you, then you'll feel better. All this huff and gruff you're hearing from me is bull."

He went around and helped her down, he was holding her arm when she said, "No, I don't have any clean clothes, that backpack is empty. I found it laying by the side of the road."

"I see, well let's see what we can do, I have a little extra time." Bob took her in to the truck stops store and let her find a whole new outfit with extra socks and underwear. He arranged for her a shower and sat in the truckers lounge while she took care of business.

He had really looked at her then, there was a bruise on the back of her neck that her hair hid and the windbreaker was way too big. Bob had seen a lot over the years and not much surprised him anymore. That is until she came back. She was a good looking woman he judged, about twenty five or so. Reddish brown hair and green eyes told of Irish ancestry.

She stood about five foot eight and weighed about a hundred and thirty pounds or so. The clothes fit her well, jeans and a jersey top. He noticed she had no jewelry, no watch, no rings.

"Well now Sadie, I see you clean up right nicely, let's see what they got to eat in this dump." After she ate and Bob polished off a pot of black coffee she said, "I thank you, you are very kind, God must have sent you."

"God ain't got nothing to do with me, it was just bad luck on my part." He was uncomfortable, no one had spoken to him like that in . . . he couldn't remember.

"Okay, you want the story?" she asked, "Here goes, I was in Colorado Springs, my boyfriend is stationed at Fort Carson. We rented a small apartment together and I could only find work as a bartender. I don't know what happened to him but he changed. He was such a nice guy back home but now he drank every night and would want to argue and fight. Then he thought I was cheating on him while I was at work."

She sighed and looked away for a second, "Three nights ago I came home late and he was very drunk. He had trashed the apartment, smashed the windows out, and broke the door. He grabbed me by the neck and kept punching me in the stomach saying he was killing the kid because it wasn't his. I'm not pregnant now nor was I then. He took my purse and set it on fire then ran out and smashed the windows out of my car. I ran then, I ran and ran. I got a couple of rides that brought me to Wyoming, then another one to where you found me. The last guy had tried to rape me but I got away."

Bob sat there and didn't speak for a couple of minutes. "You mentioned New York, where in New York?"

"Umm, Binghamton, you ever hear of it?" she answered.

"Yeah kid, I know where it is, I'll take you there. You have folks there?" He asked gently.

"Uh, yeah, my Mom and Dad, I can pay you back when we get there, honest." She stated.

"Please, don't think of that, that would be an insult." Bob leaned back and said, "You want to call them, let them know you're alright?"

"Yeah, that would be a good idea." She nodded her head. Bob went back to the store and got her a prepaid phone card and went back to the table to give her some privacy. He felt so strange, a feeling he never felt before. He didn't tell her anything about himself, but what was there to tell? Straight to the service out of high school, then he got his first driving job. Married once for less that a year then . . . what? He had a post office box and a bank account back in Slippery Rock, he lived in his truck. Damn, he was lonely.

"Okay, I talked to them. They were worried but are happy I'm coming home." Sadie had interrupted his moody thoughts and brought him out of his reverie. He stood up and looked at her and said, "Well then let's see if Maggie can fly."

# CHAPTER FOUR

Brad Singer was on vacation. In mid October he was at his camp near Tionesta, Pa doing a little hunting, a little drinking, and his new interest prepping. He caught the prepping bug two years earlier from his buddy Phil who worked with him at the mill in Pittsburgh.

"Yeah Brad, ya never know when the shit will hit the fan and you need to bug out so you can survive." Phil told him at lunch one day. "Hell, look at that stock collapse that happened, if the fed hadn't propped them assholes up we'd all be starving right now. Everybody needs to stock up on supplies, get guns with plenty of ammo and have a plan."

"A plan," said Brad, "What kind of plan?"

"Jesus, are you dense or what? A bug out plan you idiot. You won't be safe with all these gangs and fricking thieves and shit running around. Don't look for the cops to help ya, it'll be every man for himself." Phil said nodding in that way that meant he conveyed great wisdom.

"You're crazy," Brad replied, "none of that shit is gonna happen, we've got laws, the police, the national flinking guard for Christ's sake, FEMA even."

"Oh yeah, look at how well they handled Katrina," Phil said sarcasticly "five days just to get water there. Hey, don't take my word for it, use your computer at home and look it up."

Brad did, the more he looked the more frightening it got. He was lucky, his Grandfather had bought a hunting camp in the mountains back in 1939 and it had gone to his Dad and now it was his. He loved the place, the woods were right out the back door. The Allegheny river a couple miles away and it was quiet. So quiet you could hear the quiet. The eight point he shot when he was twelve years old was mounted and hung on the wall. Pictures of his Granddad and his Dad as a kid framed and hung, even his Mom and little sister loved to come here.

Now it was just him, he and his wife divorced six years ago and they hadn't had any kids, (thank God), his Mom lived with his sister and her family in Los Angeles and rarely visited. Shit, he needed to call them soon sometime. Anyway Brad started to prep for SHTF. First he got a couple cases of Ramen noodles and some bandaids then some canned stuff at Sam's Club.

Then he watched some shows on cable about prepping, hell they had a whole series. He got serious. He cut a hole in the floor of the spare bedroom and dug a storage room. Sealed the walls, built shelves and began to stock. He got cases of MREs at the army surplus and a plastic three hundred gallon water container. This trip he put up solar panels and hooked up batteries to them. He had a 30.06 deer rifle, a twelve gauge pump, (he took the plug out and now it held five rounds instead of three) and his new toy a 41 caliber revolver with an eight inch barrel. There was even a crossbow under the bed. Plenty of candles and kerosene lamps, he felt he was ready.

There were neighbors but he had only seen them on major holidays like the fourth of July and a couple times on the first day of buck season. Usually he had the whole road to himself, not that people didn't come back in here. Jake and his wife Mary, a couple of old hippies lived close by.

Jake mowed the lawns, cut the firewood, did odd jobs and knew who to call for various reasons. He also grew the best pot Brad had ever tried, it pays to make friends with the locals.

Brad heard a car outside and looked out to see the Sheriff getting out of his jeep.

"Hello," hailed the Sheriff, "you got a couple minutes?"

"Yeah, sure," said Brad, "how can I help you?"

"Oh, I wondered if maybe you might have noticed some fellers snooping around, seems some propane tanks have been coming up missing."

Brad wiped his hand on his cammo pants and extended it to shake. "Hi, I'm Brad Singer."

"Yeah I know, I knew your Dad." The Sheriff said giving a firm grip.

"No sir, I haven't seen anyone like that and my tanks are okay." Brad jerked his head towards the camp.

"Well okay, but keep a watch, they took four tanks just down German Hill road and I think we got a couple of wildcat dope cookers around the area." The Sheriff said with a serious note. "You notice any funny smells?"

"Uh, no sir, just my campfire or my cooking," Brad said.

"Well okay," the Sheriff held out a card, "Jake down the road said he's seen a little black car driving around lately. If you notice one would you give me a call?"

"Oh yeah sure, no problem, well I got to get to work. I'm cutting firewood for my wood burner."

The Sheriff gave a little goodbye wave and got back in his jeep, backed around and left. Brad went over to one of his two sheds and unlocked the door. In this one was the old four wheeler and trailer his Dad got when those things first came out.

You had to wind a rope and pull it to get it started but it still ran good even if it leaked a little oil. Granddad had paid five hundred dollars for two five acre lots way back when and now there were trails in there that went for miles.

Brad placed the chainsaw, gas and oil in the trailer, wound his rope and fired it up. A big puff of blue smoke came out but cleared up after it warmed up. His property butted up on the national forest and the woods were thick for miles

It was okay to pick up fallen branches and to cut up dead trees, besides, he had a permit. It was a good kind of work and Brad liked doing it and hey, he had a week and a half of vacation left.

His buddies thought he picked an odd time of year to take it but he loved the autumn in the forest.

# CHAPTER FIVE

The chain reaction in the sun caused by the exploding object created a vortex of swirling superheated gasses. They came into contact with a mass of cooler plasma. The resulting storm turned into a type of solar tornado that erupted in a coronal mass ejection of violent geomagnetic disturbances stronger than the Carrington event of 1859.

This came off the sun directly in line with the Earth. It would strike the planet in three days. NASA sent a coded message to the White House and held its breath.

The next day was when Ho Lin was happy, his daughter was wed, his new in-laws were content with the feast of chicken and rice, only he felt a little tickle in his throat.

Everyone gathered for the wedding pictures. After they were taken Ho Lin asked them to please remain where they were for a short moment. He wished to make a speech.

He faced them and as he spoke he began to feel very hot and then began to sneeze. The wedding party tried to be polite but when Ho Lin fell towards them vomiting they broke away. The mutated avian flu had infected them all.

The goodbyes were hurriedly said and the newlyweds and in-laws fled for Bejing. In two hours Ho Lin was dead, his wife in delirium. The infected were getting sick at the wedding reception near the airport.

This made the Spanish Influenza seem like a mild cold. The death rate was ninety eight percent within thirty six hours of infection, most never lived that long.

A few hours later it was on its way around the world in several jet airliners. Bejing was in panic mode, people fleeing the city in droves, for all of them it was too late.

Rusty wasn't feeling so hot. He awoke about three in the morning. He made it to the toilet and puked, he also had diarrhea. He couldn't get up he slipped and fell in the mess. He began to shake like he was having an epileptic attack. His last conscious thought was that he was very hungry.

Mad cow disease destroys the frontal lobes of the brain. The parts that control reason, thought, rationality and fine balance. The body still functions but not on a human level.

The morning sun found Rusty wandering into Hays, Kansas. Staggering like a drunk only one goal in mind, to eat.

Larry Finn was on his way to work, he was the cook at the Hays Dinor. He always arrived early and got the prep work done so when they opened at six am breakfast was ready and the coffee was hot.

He pulled into the back of the place and walked to the rear door. He saw Rusty at the last second, his eyes blood red and groaning.

What used to be Rusty, a good old bubba, flung himself at Larry and started biting. Larry got away and ran screaming to the main street of town.

Officer John Laughlin left his patrol car and ran to the distressed man to see what was wrong. He forced Larry to the pavement and saw the bloody bite marks but before he could ask what happened Larry began to convulse and the whites of his eyes filled with blood.

Then he began to bite also. Officer Laughlin got free and ran to his patrol car and radioed for help. Townspeople came to see what was going on and were bitten also trying to give aid.

Some people didn't succumb right away and fled in cars to try and get to the hospital. Some made it, and the hospital was soon destroyed.

In two hours the infected were spreading out in a circle from Hays, racing away as fast as they could. At this point for some inexplicable reason, the virus mutated again. Now it did not affect the balance part of the brain, they infected could now run.

This was when the CME hit the Earth.

# CHAPTER SIX

T wo days prior the president was in a meeting in a very secure room under the white house. Thirty two people were present, the joint chiefs of staff, the vice president, speaker of the house and the entire cabinet.

The head of the department of homeland security spoke first. "Mr. President, I have been informed by NASA that we are about to experience a coronal mass ejection from the sun with more force than any in recorded history."

"What exactly does that mean?" asked the President.

He sat down and another man stood up. "Well Sir, we know that one hit the Earth in 1859 and was known as the Carrington Event. It caused sparks to erupt from telegraph receivers and melted the one eighth inch copper wires that connected them."

The Presidents scientific advisor stated and continued, "This event will be three times more powerful and will not only disrupt the electrical grid but will destroy all unprotected electronic devices from cell phones to guidance systems. The world will be pushed back to the early 1840s, the days of the pony express."

"I see," said the President, "what can we do?"

The national security advisor stood up. "Sir, we must evacuate the government to our newly finished, secure underground facility beneath the Denver airport. There are provisions for five thousand personnel for up to five years. Also our underground road and rail network is complete and we can move directly from here to most points in the country. All in all Sir, we can assure the safety of ninety thousand people for up to three years."

"Gentlemen and ladies, we shall enact plan 'Operation Freedom'. I assume you can proceed with all haste." The President asserted but then asked, "But what about the American people?"

The director of the DHS spoke up again, "Sir, your family and the families of everyone in this room will be protected. Once we seal off the entrances to the system no one can breach them. As long as the government can survive we can guarantee the continuity of the United States of America."

"We foresee mass rioting and bloodshed," this from the head of FEMA, "also Sir, we cannot hope to deal with an emergency of this scale. After all, we're talking about three hundred million people in this country alone. Not to mention over half of them will be armed."

"Well," said the President, "it appears we have less than forty eight hours to secure our positions. I have many phone calls to make there will be no press leaks people. Issue the appropriate orders and may God help us."

The underground facilities had been under construction since the beginning of the cold war. At first just mere shelters under large buildings, it expanded to an interconnected system of silos deep under the surface. These facilities contained everything from tons of non-perishable food and bottled water to bowling alleys. All built secretly on the taxpayers dime.

Only the elite, the elected and their immediate families along with only healthy, young military personnel were slated for entrance.

The plan had been worked on for years, long before the current president was in office. When the time was right they were going to cause a major world financial collapse and in the ensuing riots martial law would be declared.

Then they would simply round up anyone classified as non-contributing, place them in FEMA camps and exterminate them until the population of the world fell below five hundred million. Just as it was cut on the Georgia Guide Stones.

Then they would emerge and take control of the entire planet, granting themselves Godlike status. It was a good plan, it was good for America, it was good for the world.

Powered by thermal vents drilled deep into the Earth and incorporating air recycling systems including artificially lit gardens for fresh fruits and vegetables they were for the most part self sustaining.

State of the art medical facilities were in place in key areas of the network. Very well planned and constructed for a government project.

Now a better option had arisen. At the same time the President had given his orders Ho Lin was killing his chickens and a certain cow found freedom.

# CHAPTER SEVEN

Arnie was watching his router cut its patterns when the power shut off. There was a big bang from outside as the main transformer blew and caught fire.

Big Mike was yelling for everyone to clear the building as a fire broke out behind the shaper machine. The maintenance man ran by with a fire extinguisher and sprayed it on the burning electric box.

Arnie calmly grabbed his lunch and thermos and walked outside. The transformer on the pole was blazing away and he could see smoke rising from several places. They were all supposed to meet at the parking lot in case of fire and had just ran a drill the week before.

"Looks like we're done for today," Mike said, "they probably won't get that fixed until tomorrow." That's when the wires burst into flame and started falling.

"Holy crap, there's fires all over the place!" one of the guys hollered. Sure enough, wires were burning and falling everywhere, smoke was coming from several buildings.

"Mike!" Bill Gant yelled, "I got to go to the firehouse, they'll be needing me." Mike waved him off. Bill got in his truck but it wouldn't start.

"Somebody give him a ride." Mike shouted and Jerry Kline tried his car. "It won't start either, what's going on here?"

Nobodies car started except old Sam's sixty eight GMC. "Come on Bill, I got ya, this old gal never let me down yet." Sam shouted.

As they drove off Mike said, "Me and Harry will stay here and watch for fires. If you guys want to go and see if anybody needs help, go next door first then check those houses. Be damn careful and don't touch those power lines.

They rushed off, Arnies lunch and thermos forgotten on the hood of his chevy. They fought the small fires with whatever they could find but it was a wasted effort.

People were running in and out trying to save stuff, Arnie and Jerry got an old lady out of her bungalow then went back in for her two cats.

Sam came driving back and stopped when he saw Arnie. "I got Bill to the fire station but none of the trucks would start an dthe fire house was burning. Is this some kind of a terrorist attack?"

"I don't know Sam, I don't know, hey, try the radio." Arnie pointed to his dash. Sam turned it on but there was nothing but static. He turned the dial and caught 'enerator on and can continue broadcasting. It appears there is a major power outage in the listening area. We will try to learn more but the phone service also seems to be out.'

Arnie pulled his cell phone out of his pocket but it wouldn't even light up. 'Achey Breaky Heart' started to play on the radio and Sam shut it off. "Hate that damn song," he said, "and what a little whore his kid turned out to be."

Smoke was swirling all around them, people were yelling and screaming. "Sam, forget that, what the heck are we gonna do?" Arnie shouted.

"Don't know about you but I'm going home, my missus will be shitting bricks and my place could be burning too. Arnie, did you try your car?"

"Yeah, it won't start either." He shook his head.

"You want a ride? You know I go right past your place." Sam offered.

"Yeah, if somebody wants my lunch they can have it."

Jerry spoke up then, "I'll go back and tell Mike where you went, I'm sure it'll be okay." Arnie nodded and climbed into the pickup, Sam hit the gas.

It was slow going, all the cars and trucks were stopped and a lot of folks didn't get them off the road. Fires were everywhere, luckily it started raining buckets but it made driving worse.

As they neared Tionesta they came up by the elementary school and Arnie saw the kids crowded around the entrance trying to stay dry.

"Sam, you think we could stop and get my boy?" Arnie asked.

"Oh yeah, your kid sure. My place is probably burnt to the ground by now anyways."

They pulled in and Arnie jumped out and ran up to the crowd. "Clay! Clay! Where's Clay Swende?"

"Here Dad," and Clay pushed his way out.

"Are you that boy's father?" one of the teachers called out, "because if you're not I can't let him go."

"Yes, Mrs. Rictor, he's my Dad." Clay answered her.

"Okay then, you go on. Have you heard anything Sir? Do you know what's going on?"

"No Ma'am, only that the power is out all over and none of the cars will run." Arnie answered her as he put a protective arm around his son.

"Goodness me, I wonder how we'll get the children home?" she asked, turning to one of the other teachers.

"I don't know Ma'am but I'm sure help will come." Arnie said over his shoulder as he got Clay in the truck. That's when he realized that Sam's old truck was the only thing they saw moving on the road.

"Why do think this old piece of crap is the only thing running?" He asked Sam.

"Points," Sam said with a finger in the air, "points, this thing doesn't have any of that electronic ignition stuff. I bet we were attacked. A nuke blowing up in the sky would do this. I was watching one of those doomsday shows and this is what they said would happen if somebody set a nuke off in the atmosphere. It makes sense, anyway it won't be running long. I'm low on gas and only got a little less than a gallon at home. Can't stop at the gas station, no power."

"I got almost five in my tractor can in the shed, you're welcome to it." Arnie said.

They pulled up to Arnie's house and it was still there. Mattie was on the porch holding a shovel and Goofy ran up to the truck barking. Arnie and his son got out and Clay ran to his mother saying, "Mom, mom, the power went out at the school and we had to go outside and it rained really, really hard."

"I know honey." She replied, "I managed to put a fire out with this shovel. The power lines broke and fell against the side of the house. They were burning, so I grabbed up this shovel and threw dirt on them 'til they went out. How was your day dear?"

Sam had got out by then and walked around the truck. Arnie couldn't believe how calm she was, like this stuff was an everyday thing.

"Well, chaotic to say the least." Sam nudged him, "I'm thinking about those kids at the school and how they will get home. Do you think your Massey-Ferguson will start?"

Arnie blinked, "Well, if what you say is true then yes, it will start, why?"

"What are you two cooking up, Sam?" Mattie asked.

"Well," said Sam, "if my place is still standing and Becca is okay then we'll run your tractor over, hook up that big hay wagon of mine, toss a couple bales on and give those kids an old fashioned hay ride home."

"Yeah, yeah, that's an idea. If Mattie has no objection, I got a big tarp in case it rains again." He looked at Mattie who shrugged and rolled her eyes.

"men love to be boys, come on kiddo there's some cookies in there to go with your milk." And mother and son went in the house.

The tractor was an antique that Arnies Uncle left him. To start it you had to set the spark and use a hand crank. It fired right up on the second try. The tank was already full and Sam put the spare gas in his truck and they were ready to go the half mile to Sam's place.

Clay was drinking his milk and feeding chunks of peanut butter cookies to Goofy when Arnie walked in.

"Honey look, I know this has been an unusual day and this trip to the school is probably going to be for naught but if those kids are stranded . . . ."

"Go, don't worry about us, we'll be fine, ain't that right Clay?" Mattie smiled.

"Uh, I better take a flashlight, don't know how long this will take and that tractor goes slow." Arnie gave her a peck on the cheek and ruffled Clay's hair as he walked out the door. Twenty minutes later they were hooking up the trailer.

"Becca is going to stay at your house, she doesn't want to be alone. She can drive the truck down and here, I got us an Oklahoma credit card." He said as he tossed a can and hose on the trailer with a grin.

The trip was not in vain, they got back to the school about a half an hour before it would have let out and there had been no help that came by.

There was one teacher watching them pull in and they both walked up to her. "Excuse us Ma'am but have you heard anything from anybody yet?" Sam asked her.

"No we haven't. You're the only people we've seen go by all day now." Mrs. Rictor said, "I for the life of me am getting worried, none of our cars will start, the phone doesn't work, and no busses have arrived."

"We figured that, the only things that seem to run are antiques like this tractor. We wish to volunteer to take the kids and I guess you teachers home if you're ready." Sam told her.

The teachers held a quick conference and let those students go who could walk home. They figured it wasn't like they would get ran over by any trucks or drunk drivers today. The rest of the kids got on the hay ride and started throwing it around.

They had to go about ten miles in a sort of circle but when they got to the first house where the twins lived there was a problem. The house was burnt down. The family car was in the driveway so Sam went to take a look around.

"You boys will just have to come along with us tonight," he said as he got back, "I left a note on the cars window for your folks. They must not be here." Sam shot a look at Arnie and climbed back on.

That happened twice more before they dropped the last child off to grateful parents. Sam held his peace and acted cheerful towards the kids on the wagon.

There were four kids still on the wagon when they got back to Arnies. Sam had told Arnie that he saw bodies in the ashes but figured not to tell the kids just yet. Arnie looked at the three boys and the one girl who just so happened to be Sally Pinker.

# CHAPTER EIGHT

Sadie was in the sleeper, thirty miles into what Bob Seeger immortalized as 'that long and lonely highway east of Omaha' Sadie was yawning and Bob made her go lie down. She was asleep in minutes.

Bob was wasting no time tonight, he had a mission. The load was due in Piscataway, New Jersey on Friday, it was Monday night now. Lots of time, he could have taken it easy but this was a different thing now. He felt an uneasiness, an urgency, he was totally alert.

He would top off his tanks before he crossed the Mississippi as he wouldn't find cheaper fuel east of there. He was running with two other trucks all doing eighty-five, the cb was on but nobody felt like talking which suited him just fine. He had to think.

What had happened to Sadie happened to a lot of women, hell, men too for that matter. But she had guts, that was for sure.

This could be a con job but he didn't think so, he watched her eyes when she spoke. They said she wasn't lying.

That thing she said about God having sent him was bothersome. He didn't know God from Pee Wee Herman, never gave it much thought. Thinking however, was one thing he was good at.

He found the answers to many of life's mysteries and all the world's problems. But him being an instrument of God's will, well, that was crazy, plain nuts.

Well enough of that crap he thought and slipped a Creedence cd in the player, that always made him feel better.

Sadie was in the woods being chased by something evil, unspeakable. Fear gripped her with icy claws. She felt like she was running in thick gravy, she was going too slow, it was going to catch her any second. She was falling, falling, falling . . .

She awoke with a start, disoriented at first then she remembered where she was. Damn, she had to pee.

"Good morning," said Bob, as she slipped into the jump seat and fastened her seat belt.

"Can we stop soon? I gotta go." Sadie said with a vacant 'I'm not awake yet' stare out the windshield.

"You, young lady are in luck, Maggie is thirsty and she likes to drink at the next exit coming up in a minute and a half." Bob said in a polite curtly voice.

"Good," said Sadie, still staring out the front.

Bob started to slow down, took the exit and pulled up to the pumps at the Pilot. Sadie wasted no time getting her shoes on and bolting for the door.

Bob got out and stretched, felt his joints crack, opened his side compartment and got out his gloves. No one fueled his truck but him.

With his white towel in hand so not a drop fell on his shining tanks he carefully started the pump then went around to the other side and repeated the process. $1014.00 later he went in to pay.

Sadie was staring at the coffee pots and he said, "Go ahead and get a cup, and me too, large and black. Find a seat over there, I got to move the truck."

Bob soon came back in and went to the restroom, fifteen minutes later he joined her at the tiny table.

"If you're hungry grab a donut or something." She shook her head no but said, "I could use a refill."

"Get it," Bob said as he adjusted his black cowboy hat, "but mind your bladder. This ain't no family vacation tour."

"I'll be just fine." She said primly but only got a half a cup. They sat in silence after that. Bob noticed the sky in the east was beginning to lighten.

"You ready? It's time to go." He said rising out of the plastic chair. She grabbed his empty cup and threw both in the trash.

In the truck she noticed the fuel receipt laying on the floor and picked it up. "A thousand dollars?" she said with astonishment.

"Plus the coffee," Bob grinned, "now you know why a bag of potato chips cost four bucks. They add that tax on a heavy as their salaries can stand it. That cost is eventually paid by the consumer, you and me, who gets taxed again when buying it at the inflated prices. Quite a racket the government has going on and nobody seems to care.

Hell, the damn mafia is fairer than that." Bob said as he opened a prescription bottle and took one small white pill.

He saw her looking at him and said, "Blood pressure, its a little high without this stuff. I have to pass a physical every year and high blood pressure is a no no."

"Yeah my Dad . . ."

"Now take cigarettes for example," Bob interrupted, as he pulled back on the interstate shifting gears without even thinking about it, 'What does a pack of Camels cost now? What, seven, eight bucks? Without tax they would be ninety-eight cents. Everybody got their fingers in that pie. Oh, hey, not to mention . . .

Sadie let him pontificate and watched the sunrise. It had been a long time since she had seen one, it was so beautiful.

They crossed the Mississippi into Illinois and Bob kept right on yakking. She figured he really never had much chance to talk to someone.

"And that idiot Rush Limberger or whatever his name is said . . ." Sadie smiled and thought he really was a nice guy.

In Joliet they left the interstate and traveled east on US 30. Bob said I-80 was a toll road for a long ways and he'd be damned if he was going to pay to do his job.

It was a little slower going through towns and such but they still made good time. They were at a truck stop somewhere in Ohio that had a statue of a buffalo in the front of the building.

The news was on the tv up on the wall and was running a story about a flu epidemic in China when the power went out.

Bob watched in amazement as a transformer blew outside and caught fire. The wires lit up and started to fall.

There was a scream from the kitchen and a shout of "Fire! Call 911!" the cash register girl picked up the phone and started pushing buttons then held it down and stared stupidly at it.

"Phones dead." She said to a waitress standing next to her.

Luckily they had been lingering over their coffee and Bob grabbed the check, pulled a twenty out of his pocket and gave it to their waitress and told her, "Better get everybody out of the building right now!"

He took Sadie by the arm and said, "Let's go, now!" they made it outside getting jostled and bumped by all the other fleeing patrons as smoke filled the restaurant.

The scene outside was astonishing. Power poles were burning at their tops, wires were burning on the ground, no traffic was moving. He could hear starters cranking but that was it.

Everything was stopped, something else was odd also but he just couldn't put his finger on it.

Sadie said. "Listen Bob, there are no sirens." That was it! There should have been sirens all over the place.

"Let's go to the truck and see if she'll start." Bob said as he was swiveling his head trying to look everywhere at once.

He unlocked the passenger door and told Sadie to get in and lock it quick. He hurried around to the driver's side.

Smoke was pouring out of the restaurant and there was a muffled explosion inside, people began to scream.

He opened his door and three quick steps he was in. as soon as he sat down he felt a sharp, stabbing pain in his chest. He took a few deep breaths and felt better.

"You okay?" Sadie was looking at him with concern, "You look a little pale."

"Ahh just a lot of excitement, I'm an old fart ya know?" he forced himself to smile at her.

"Bob, what if it doesn't start?" Sadie was looking scared.

"Well, then this is home sweet home and we become Oheezians." He turned the key and Maggie roared to life.

# CHAPTER NINE

Kansas state patrol officer Pat Coffey was pissed, the damn cruiser wouldn't start. He had the hood up but nothing seemed wrong.

Officer Sheila Smart came out of the barracks and asked sweetly, "Problems Pat? Want me to fix it?"

"Everybody likes a little ass Sheila but nobody likes a SMART ass." Pat grinned, "No, it just won't start."

"Well ta ta, I got a whole big highway to patrol." She said as she got into the other cruiser. It didn't start either.

She keyed her mike and asked for assistance but realized the radio was dead. "Hey Pat, you think somebody is playing a joke on us?" she asked as she got out and stared at the car.

Pat reached in and tried his radio too, nothing. "Let's see Joleen in dispatch, maybe something's wrong."

They walked around the front of the brick building. "Hey the generator is running, the power must be out." Sheila pointed at the steel maintenance shed where the steady hum of the powerful diesel generator was coming from.

Pat opened the door to dispatch and smelled the odor of burnt flesh and hair. Joleen Nagy, the day dispatcher was sprawled across the radio desk, tendrils of smoke rising from her head.

"JOLLEN!" Sheila screamed. "what on Earth." Joleen wasn't going to answer that or any other questions ever again. The headphones on her ears were melted and what was left of her hair was pointed straight out.

"Damn," said Pat, "it looks like the radio shorted out and fried her."

"I'll call for an ambulance and let Wichita barracks know 911 is out here." Sheila picked up the phone, frowned, hit the disconnect button a couple of times and hung it back up.

"Dead," She looked at Pat, "can we go back outside please, the smell . . ."

"Yes we can." Pat agreed, "Poor Joleen, she was going to go to Florida next month see her new granddaughter."

"Sad," Sheila said, "hey look Pat, there's something burning over there by the pole." They both looked at the downed wires.

"What do you make of this, Officer Smart?"

"I am not an electrician Officer Coffey but I would venture to say that there was one big flecken short somewhere."

The state patrol barracks they were stationed at was situated off I-70 on an access road about two miles from the exit.

There was a deserted house nearby but the closest neighbor was a half mile to the north. The power must have went out when they were in the locker rooms as Pat remembered the lights blinking off and coming back on a few seconds later.

They heard a noise and saw a woman and a child coming towards them crouched over like they were stalking something.

"Can I help you ma'am?" Officer Smart called out. The two began to run towards them with their arms outstretched.

Pat leapt away as the little boy dove at him snapping his jaws. Pat saw the blood on the kids back then looked at his face as he sprang back up and snarled. The eyes were blood red and the kid charged again.

He pulled his nightstick and jammed it into the little boy's chest, the kid bit it! He kept trying to force his way around the stick but Pat held him off.

He heard Sheila yelling at the woman then there was a shot. Then another and the kid fell in the dirt squirming and kicking, his leg bleeding and crippled.

The kid still tried to get at him like the wound didn't hurt.

"PAT! Get away from him!" Sheila screamed. Pat looked and saw Sheila shuffling backwards away from the woman who was crawling after her.

He ran over beside her and said, "What the heck? You shot that kid, her too?"

"Pat, they're like that guy in Florida that was on the news. The one who tried to eat that bums face off. They had to shoot him in the head to get him to stop."

"Okay Sheila, look we just can't kill them, they aren't armed." Pat had his sidearm out now also and was pointing it back and forth as they kept retreating.

"Well I got a throw down on my ankle, what about you?" Sheila yelled.

Pat stopped. "HALT! HALT OR I WILL SHOOT TO KILL!" they both kept coming. Pat and Sheila fired at the same time, both shots to the head. The attackers were dead.

Sheila spun around and vomited, Pat approached the bodies. He saw bite marks on the woman's arm and some of the flesh missing.

Jesus Sheila, a woman and a little kid. How are we gonna explain this?"

"Pat, PAT! We need to get help, let's try your truck." They tried both personal vehicles, no luck.

"Let's walk to McMurdy's it's the closest place." Sheila said. "What is going on?" cried Pat, "what the hell is going on?"

"It's like some zombie apocalypse or something." Sheila said. They looked at each other then went back to their cruisers, removed the shotguns from the front and got the AR-15s from the trunks. They put on the body armor and loaded the weapons. Then they walked north on the service road.

Elmo McMurdy had what at one time could have been called a farm. Actually it had been a nice farm when his Daddy was still alive. Now it was gone to seed, the only thing Elmo even cared about was his horses.

Bred by his Daddy for racing he did have an interest in them. At least he would sell the colts when they came of age.

He had one stallion, two geldings and six mares. He would like to sell the geldings and he was sure of at least two colts come next spring.

He didn't know the power was off, he hadn't had any for two years. The damn power company kept sending him bills even if paid one once in a while. One day it didn't work anymore but they still sent those cotton picking bills those dirty sons of bitches.

He heard the dogs barking and perked up, maybe he had a cash buyer.

Pat knocked on the door of the house while the dogs raised holy hell.

"Hold on, hold on, I'm coming." He opened the door with a smile on his face which dropped like a brick down a well when he saw the two heavily armed state troopers.

"Lorda mercy, I ain't stole nuttin in a long, long time. I learnt my lesson, yes I did, I surely did." He exclaimed with both hands in the air.

"Elmo, take it easy, can you shut these dogs up?" Officer Coffey asked.

Elmo looked at both troopers, licked his lips, inserted two fingers in his mouth and blew one of the loudest whistles a man could make.

Pat and Sheila both winced but the dogs shut up and ran off towards the barn. Elmo looked back at the officers and grinned. He looked a lot like Alphalfa on the original 'Our Gang' series with that same cow lick on the crown of his head.

"How can I hep you today?" he asked as politely as he could.

"Elmo McMurdy, the Great State of Kansas needs your help," Sheila said, "we need transportation."

"Transpo, transpo, po . . ."

"Elmo! We need two horses with saddles and bridles." Pat said a little testily. Elmo looked at them like they were crazy then thought a minute.

"I would truly like to hep the Great State of Kansas but I'm a businessman and horse's is my business, I just can't give them away." He nodded his head at both of them.

"We figured that Elmo, we will write you a receipt that you can take to the courthouse in Hays to get paid with." Officer Smart assured him.

"The same courthouse that sent me to Topeka for two years over a small misunderstanding?"

"Yes Elmo, the same one." Pat said.

"What if I say no?"

"Then we shoot you and take them anyway." Sheila said with a smile resting her shotgun on her shoulder.

Elmo looked to the left. He looked to the right. Then he said with a great big smile. "Officers, you got a deal, write that note for ten thousand dollars. The two geldings are in the corral and fine horses they are too."

Surprisingly, they were.

# CHAPTER TEN

Sunday night at the airport in Hilo, Hawaii was slow. Stan Shawgo was bored and getting restless. His flight to Denver had been delayed for who knows why and he'd been waiting for three hours now.

A navy man, excuse me, an ex-navy man having been honorably discharged earlier that day. He longed to see the Rocky Mountains again. He had seen all the water he wanted to see, now he couldn't wait to lay on a big red rock that didn't move.

He decided to walk around the terminal again, there were some hot babes here even if they did have boyfriends or husbands.

He was down by baggage claim when a flight arrived from Taiwan. He sat on a bench and watched the passengers disembark.

Lots of Asians, a couple walked by talking with a British accent, cool. A very properly dressed young lady came by, stopped in front of him and sneezed.

The loud speaker sounded and his flight was finally being called, he jumped up, almost colliding with that pretty young lady who sneezed again. She had nice perfume on.

Stan rushed to the gate, went through security and handed his boarding pass to the lady at the ramp. Thank God he was on his way home.

The direct flight to Denver took off, a redeye flight he planned on getting some good sleep on the not so crowded airplane. He didn't know it but there was another passenger traveling with him, a very viral passenger.

The movie was a stupid chick flick about true love and marriage. Why couldn't they show one of those fast and furious films? Yeah, fast cars, hot chicks and getting over on the bad guys, that was more his style. Finally he nodded off.

He awoke to bell chimes and the stewardess telling everyone they would be landing soon and to please fasten their seat belts. He felt a little warm and there was a tickle in the back of his throat. He hoped he wasn't coming down with a cold, that would be so unfair.

The flight ended without incident and he got off the plane. He hadn't seen the new airport before and was amused at all the creepy murals on the walls. Such bad art, he thought.

He coulda swore he saw Dick Cheney, the ex vice president but it may have been anybody.

Damn, he had to take a crap. Good, there was the men's room, he was in luck. He sneezed just as he was going in and this general was coming out.

"Excuse me sir," he said and the general said, "bless you." Imagine that a freaking general blessed him!

He was getting warm, shit, was this a fever? He flushed and zipped up, time to find his Dad who said he was picking him up.

Four star General Howard Porter was meeting his wife's flight from Dallas. He had to personally escort her to the secret entrance of the underground complex.

She was all he had now, his son had been killed by a suicide car bomber in Irac. Thirty one years in the army and he had never been in harm's way. How ironic about his son, in for less than a year.

There was his wife! Funny how much she looked like Barbra Bush. Well, she had always been a very proper wife. Keeping her safe was the least he could do. Once those doors were sealed none of the great unwashed could get in and by the time all the damned civilians killed each other off they would emerge to start a new world order without all those rights and liberal ass laws.

A Colonel approached him and saluted. "General Porter Sir, it is my privilege to escort you, Sir." He saluted back, "Carry on Colonel." Yes, discipline and order, what a fine new world we will have.

They entered the first of three locked compartments. Inside they were handed protective goggles and had to strip to the nude. He and his wife were instructed to hold their breath while disinfectant was sprayed on them from twenty different nozzles covering every inch of their skin.

That lasted only thirty seconds and then a warm rinse was applied. In the next chamber they placed their feet in a foot bath then dried them and put on clean scrubs and slippers.

A doctor appeared and sprayed the inside of their ears and had them rinse out their mouths with a minty wash.

Finally a nurse took their vital signs and they were given a new uniform for him and a new suit for her. When they were ready, they were escorted to their quarters. This procedure was done on everyone who entered. They wished to take no chances on diseases being carried in on the skin.

# CHAPTER ELEVEN

Brad got back around four in the afternoon and pulled his loaded trailer over by the chopping block. He was a little hungry and wanted a beer.

He went inside and opened the fridge, a Nordge from the fifties that still worked good. It was covered with stickers like 'squirrel hunter's got nuts,' and 'they can take my gun from my cold, dead fingers.'

The little light didn't work. He pushed the on/off button but nothing happened. He grabbed a can of Old German and the ham, cheese, and mustard, put them on the table reached over and tried the lights, nothing.

Power must be out, he thought, good. He could hook up the batteries from the solar panels and see how that went but first, 'da samach' as his Dad would have said.

He missed his Dad, dead now for ten years. Stupid heart attack. Dad had got him hired on at the mill and had trained him on the overhead crane.

Brad was proud he had never left the old man down, never gave him a reason to doubt. He hadn't got all A's in school but he got a few, never was the big quarterback but caught his fair share of passes and even scored a couple of times. He hadn't been the prom king but had looked good with Debbie Kranzinski on his arm.

Dad was busting with pride when he made his first lift and transfer with the crane and didn't kill anybody.

There was a picture of his Dad at sixteen hoisting a big walleye, Brad raised his can, "here's to you old man, you were always a good guy."

After his snack he went out back and hooked up the DC wires. On his last trip up he had ran the wires and put up car lights and even an old radio from some car he had found in Granddad's tinkering shed. There was God knew what in there. Grandpap kept everything and it was kinda fun to root around in there, ya never knew what you would find. Like that old porno picture from back in the twenties or thirties, some half ugly broad with her legs spread and a bored look on her face. He wondered if Granddad had . . .

"Hey, hello the camp!" Brad looked and there was Jake on a bicycle grinning at him.

"Hey, good to see you," said Jake, "you got power?"

"I got power in the blood dude. Ha ha, but no, no electric." Brad said smiling.

Jake was one of those people you just had to like. Long pony tail down his back, big bushy beard, tints of red and grey. Always had a twinkle in his eye and made you think that everything was funny.

"Uh huh, well ours is out too and Mary wanted to get something from town but our truck won't start and I thought if I shared this big old fatty with you, you might see it in the goodness of your heart to give us a ride. I got gas money too."

"Yeah sure, just let me see if my new contraption works or not."

Jake leaned the bike against a tree and walked up. "Whatcha got? Ooo solar panels, going green are you? That's one of my favorites."

Brad walked by him and went into the camp, found the toggle switch and there was light! "It works! How about that?" Brad stepped back, crossed his arms on his chest and admired his handicraft.

Jake lit the joint. "Ere, celebrate." He said and extended it to Brad.

Brad took a drag and started coughing, "holy shit, it tastes like a skunks ass, what do you call this stuff?"

"Good huh? Dylithium mind meld in honor of 'beam me up Scotty.'" Jake grinned.

"Cool, come on I'll give you that ride." However Brad's new Ford f250 four wheel drive, with the fancy chrome face guard and four hundred dollars apiece tires and wheels failed to start.

"I'll be damned," said Brad, "forty thousand and change and it won't start. That sleazy car dealer will not like me."

Jake took one last toke off the roach and shook his head, "And to think there Bradley, three hundred for my old piece of shit and I get the same service, doesn't seem fair, does it?" Jake was chuckling. "Well, I gotta go tell Mary the sad news that if she wants to go to town she's gonna have to peddle her ass."

Brad started to laugh, "Hey, what's up with the Sheriff? He said he talked to you."

"Yeah, he did. Seems somebody is serious about free propane. I mean really, those big ass tanks weigh a hundred pounds or more." Jake said, "I told Wolfy it was probably some dickheads cooking meth or something and if I heard a big explosion I'd give him a call. Don't matter to me if they're tramping around the woods, my harvest is in."

"I hear that," said Brad, "well, I'll keep an eye out too. I'll be up for another week or so."

"Maybe longer if your truck don't start." observed Jake.

"Oh, I'll get it towed right back to the dealer and they will pay for that bill. They won't like it, that's for sure."

Jake walked over to the bike, "Well, got to go, keep warm, it's supposed to get chilly tonight."

Brad pointed at the wood stacked on the trailer, "No problamo amigo."

Jake had the bike turned and was getting on when Brad said, "Tell Mary I said hello." Jake waved as he peddled off a little wobbly.

Damn, I'm stoned, thought Brad. I'm gonna have to get some of that shit. He looked at his truck and dug out his cell phone but there was no service, not even a light.

"Shit, doesn't anything work around here today?" Brad said to himself. He walked through the scrunchy leaves back to the camp, went inside and tried the radio. It took a minute to warm up and then . . ." 'oadcast, this is not a test. There has been a major power outage, possibly planet wide. All telephone communication is out. Citizens are asked to stay in their homes. Power is expected to be out at least one week. FEMA is working now with all power companies to restore electrical service as soon as possible. I repeat this is not a test."

Hank Jr started singing about a family tradition and Brad turned the station but got nothing but static. Planet wide? What does that mean? What the heck is going on? These thoughts ran through Brad's mind.

Station Y101 WAPA had an eccentric owner. The man had been obsessed by the cold war. He had read all about EMPs (electrical magnetic pulses), that would result from a nuclear air burst.

He learned how to protect his broadcasting equipment by constructing a Farraday box. He simply enclosed the entire station in a metal shield including his generator building.

He wrote the emergency broadcast message himself. It was just stupid luck that he was even there that day.

He wasn't sure if anyone was receiving the signal but he was a communicator and as long as he could, he would.

He didn't know only one person was listening. The station had received no word from anywhere, he was on his own. He didn't know why he even gave that message, the words just came out.

He thought for a minute about Orson Welles then thought, what the hell. I survived two battles with the FCC, piss on it.

He didn't know that the only real communicating now however, was by word of mouth.

# CHAPTER TWELVE

That night was when the looting began, since almost everyone was walking the poorer neighborhoods were the first affected.

In Detroit the liquor store at Lennox and 21$^{st}$ was hit by two men who simply smashed the front door in with a sledge hammer.

In Chicago, the owner of Brown Bottle Liquors stood in front holding a shotgun. He was gunned down by someone he never saw.

In Dallas, a jetliner fell out of the sky when the CME hit and set off a conflagration that got worse as the fire sucked in air causing a wind that fanned the flames to increasingly higher intensity.

In Birmingham a train wrecked with six tankers of nobody ever knew what, exploded and the breeze blew the smoke and fumes throughout the city. Anyone who caught even a whiff died.

It was a night of total and utter chaos. In some communities people formed up and protected each other's homes and properties.

Police were shooting anyone they saw carrying anything until they ran out of bullets and were shot down themselves.

Millions were stranded where they were, many of them miles from home. Around the world there were about twenty two thousand airplanes in flight, three made a safe landing.

Eighty million died in the first hour alone. Some people were not affected in any way. The Amish and Mennonites for some. The Inuits of Canada were treated to spectacular northern lights.

Without the light pollution some people who had never left the city saw the stars for the first time. Many people waited for help that never came.

There are one hundred and ten thousand elevators in the US alone, thousands were trapped, some in burning buildings.

In St Louis a man walked downtown hoisting a large cross, shouting about the wrath of God. Until a gang of teenagers beat him with baseball bats and then used his own cross on him in a most disturbing way.

The suburbs and outlying areas were somewhat affected but not like the inner cities. Fires raged unabated.

Hong Kong was ravaged by fire with the survivors trapped on top of the mountain. Ships at sea were dead in the water and at the mercy of the wind and waves.

Men had been stranded at work and strived to get home to their families only to find them missing.

Many of the police on duty were stranded with their disabled patrol cars and were unable to call for help. Fire departments were crippled, ambulances were useless. Those places fortunate enough to have backup generators such as hospitals were soon swamped and overwhelmed.

Gun and pawn shops were looted, banks and jewelry stores robbed. Those who tried to stop the robbers were gunned down as the perpetrators made their getaways on foot. This was happening on a global scale.

There were many who were now too sick to care as the deadly flu was spreading like wildfire.

There had been no time to alert and gather the National Guard. Army forts were locked down and in some cases strangely empty.

Prisoners rioted and broke free of confinement, except at the supermaxes, those criminals were gassed in their cells. For many the world ended on October sixteenth.

In Kansas it was worse. By nightfall Wichita, Topeka, Salina, Oklahoma City, Lawrence and Dodge were infested by the victims of the mutated cow disease.

Those who weren't killed in the initial attacks turned into vicious carriers themselves. It was spreading fast. The only thing keeping it in check was the fact that everyone was pretty much on foot.

# CHAPTER THIRTEEN

George Bluerock was hunting turkey in the old way with a bow. He crouched in the sparse brush by the small stream. All animals must drink and this was the only water for miles.

In northern Arizona on the "rez" as they called it, life for George was relaxed. His small band of family left the mixed village of traditional adobe and newer brick government houses to live apart, as his Grandfather had been told to do in a vision.

Deep in this remote canyon they found ruins of the old ones near a tiny stream and rebuilt the ancient home.

At the age of ten George was becoming more independent and played a vital role in the family life.

Two evenings before, the whole family was present when the blue kachina doll that was kept on a shelf, fell for no reason. It landed upright and stood unaided on the floor. His Grandfather considered this a great omen and performed several rituals.

As George practiced his patience in what little shade there was he felt a small sensation in his head. Like a feather lightly brushing his skin.

He began to have a vision. A man dressed in white with pure white hair was smiling at him. He felt a sense of peace and family from the man. In images, the man warned that he and his family must stay at their home for awhile.

The turkey forgotten, he ran home. Wearing only a breechcloth, deer skin moccasins and a cloth tied around his head, he told his

Mother what had happened. She took him to his Grandfather who listened intently to the lad.

"We must follow the advice of your vision and not venture from our canyon," he said, "I do not know why but we shall remain here."

He arose and beckoned George to follow him. He led him to a path that George had never noticed before. "The old one's trail." Was what Grandfather told him.

It was faint and unused for many years. He was led up the incline, at times the ledge was very narrow. It led into a small open area within the rocks where strange figures were scratched in the stone.

His Grandfather explained the petroglyphs, that men had rode the flying birds and were friends of those who made these marks. The sun was depicted and many dead men.

At this time George's head was filled with visions from children's eyes around the world. Some showed sickness, some of adults in a panic urging their children into hiding and one of a young girl smiling at him. He felt their fear, their anguish, their deaths.

When he wished the visions to stop they did but he now understood what was happening. "We will be safe Grandfather," he told the old man, "the others will come in good time."

His Grandfather removed the amulet that proved his rank of shaman and placed it around the boy's neck. "You are the future of the Hopi," the old man said.

# CHAPTER FOURTEEN

There were nine people at Arnie's house for dinner that night. He and Sam brought in armloads of good split oak and got the wood burner in the living room to put off welcome heat.

Mattie had a propane stove so her and Becca were busy with the meal. Mattie was glad to have Becca, it was almost like having her Mom with her.

Aside from Sally Pinker there was nine year old Jimmy Kent and the eleven year old twins, Barry and Terry Blackstone. Clay sat with Sally close to the stove.

Arnie and Sam went outside to talk. "Sam, what are we gonna tell those kids about their parents and Jimmy's grandparents?" Arnie asked as he held the funnel for the kerosene lamp.

"The truth, what else?" said Sam, "The real question is what are we gonna do with them?"

"Well, I think we see how much gas we can scrounge up around here, then see if we can find Wolfy, see what he thinks. He needs to know about the bodies anyway." Arnie said as he placed the funnel back on the shelf.

The lamps were full and they screwed the tops on making sure the wicks were in the oil. "It's going to be dark soon and I bet we get a frost tonight, full moon and all." Sam said, then added, "The missus brought a pie and about a gallon of milk, a few other things too."

"You know Sam, the more I think about it I don't think it was any bomb or terrorists. I didn't notice any big flash of light, did you?"

"No, I didn't but we were in the shop, who knows? Maybe something came out of the sun, maybe something to do with that super nova that was on the news.

Maybe aliens shot us with some kind of death ray or something, hell, we may never know." Sam stood there shaking his head.

They went over to the truck and tried the radio again but there was nothing but static. "Let's get these lamps in the house and tell the kids they gotta be careful not to knock them over, damn good thing I took a notion last week to get the kero or else we'd be sitting around a birthday candle tonight."

Arnie was talking but Sam was thinking. "You know this power is gonna be out for a long time, maybe you ought to burn only one lamp tonight."

"I don't know, Sam, I don't know. There's an awful lot to think about. We'll put off telling the kids about their folks 'til after we see Wolfy, if we can find him." Sam nodded and they went in the house.

In the kitchen dinner was almost done, gulash and corn, bread, jelly, and apple pie.

The adults used the table and the kids found spots in the living room. Goofy got let outside with a bowl of dog food and a little gulash mixed in.

There wasn't much conversation, Sally wondered what she was going to wear to school tomorrow and all the boys cheered when Mattie said there was no school tomorrow.

"They can't have school without the 'letrick, can they Mrs. Swende?" asked Jimmy.

"No they can't, but give them time and they will think of something." That statement was met with groans.

After dinner the ladies were heating water to wash the dishes, Arnie had a hand pump just off the back porch and the water was good and clear.

Sam and Arnie took the twins out to help carry in more wood, it was dark now and getting colder fast.

Sally and Clay were talking quietly on the couch and Jimmy was watching the women work.

"But Sally, how can you know that? Nobody has said anything yet." Clay whispered to her.

"Because I do know," she said, "all of a sudden I can almost hear what people are thinking. I know Mom and Gus are dead." She scrunched her face at Clay, "You can too if you try, now just listen."

She looked straight in his eyes and he answered, "Yeah, I can hear you. It's like your voice is in the middle of my head. Okay I will." He stopped talking and just looked at her.

Sally started to giggle, "I knew it, I knew you liked me." She smiled.

Clay's face got red but Sally said quickly, "WE mussent tell anyone, it will be our secret, now let's practice."

Mutating viruses wasn't the only thing the gamma rays did. Armloads of wood came through the door and were stacked neatly by the stove.

Arnie called out to Mattie, "Honey, did you give any thought to where everybody's sleeping tonight?"

"Sally can have my bed, Mom," Clay piped up, "I can sleep right here." Clay patted the couch.

"Well aren't you the little gentleman? Okay, Sam and Becca get the guest room, all you boys can camp out in the living room." Mattie said with a nod of approval to herself.

"There's no tv," Terry almost whined, "what are we gonna do 'til bedtime?"

"Shut up dork," and Barry punched him in the arm.

"Hey now, enough of that." Said Mattie, "when was the last time you kids played Monopoly?"

"Monopoly!" said Becca, "I'll play, I'll be the banker and I get the hat."

"I'm the car," Jimmy said raising his hand. Mattie got the game down and the twins argued about who got the dog.

Clay said he and Sally wanted to talk some more. Sally nodded and they sat back on the couch with their heads close together.

Arnie said, "Come on Sam, I'll show you my new drill in the basement. There might even be a beer or two down there too."

So that was how things were at the Swende house that night while not far away insanity ruled the night.

# CHAPTER FIFTEEN

Bob got it in gear and pulled out, almost hitting a man who ran in front of him. There was a rig blocking the exit of the parking lot but Bob was able to go around it and got on the road headied to the on ramp.

He reached up and turned on the CB but it didn't work, the radio wouldn't come on either. He made a noise to express his disgust and put his attention to the road.

The interstate was lined with cars and trucks, most of which had made it to the berm. There were a few accidents.

As he headed towards Akron he told Sadie to get back in the sleeper and look in the drawer under the bunk. "What do you want?" she asked.

"There's a gun in there and some spare shells. Be careful, don't touch the trigger, it's loaded. Bring it up here and put it on the floor." Bob said calmly as he avoided a stalled four wheeler.

People were standing by the road looking under hoods and some were waving for him to stop but he ignored them.

"For some reason we're the only thing running, we can't stop or we'll get mobbed." Bob continued in a calm voice, "if I have to slow way down or stop for some reason and somebody jumps up and tries the door, you show them the gun."

It was a twelve gauge pump home defender model with a pistol grip. "That should discourage them." Bob added.

Sadie looked at the gun laying on the floor and asked, "What if it doesn't?"

"Then you hand it to me grip first and dive back there." Bob jerked his thumb towards the sleeper.

He had to drop it clear down to third and go on the median to avoid a wreck. "I reckon the road's are gonna be blocked up in Akron so we're going to do a little sightseeing on the back roads soon."

Sadie looked out the window and saw three houses burning and people running around. "I don't know if I want to see those sights." She said with a note of fright in her voice.

"I wish the CB worked," said Bob, "I hate driving while blind."

Bob took I-76 to Akron, stayed on straight for a short hop on I-277 which broke down to route 224. The going wasn't bad but he kept it under forty which was maddening but prudent.

He drove on to Berlin Center then turned north. They saw one car moving, a sixty four Ford Galaxy pouring smoke out the exhaust with an elderly couple in it.

They made it back to I-76 and turned up the on ramp. There was a state patrol officer walking down the ramp. He made motions for Bob to stop then started to reach for his sidearm. Bob mashed the foot feed and blew his horn.

He had got the horn from a feller that had worked on the railroad and that baby was one loud S.O.B. the cop had sense enough to jump out of the way and Bob started to chuckle. "I always wanted to do that, hee hee." They passed the stalled cruiser with its lights flashing and soon drove on to I-80.

They crossed the state line at Sharon and the passing lane was open for a few miles. They had just passed the Barkeyville exit when they had to stop.

Trucks were overturned, cars were smoking from a burned out mess. One man leapt up on the passenger side and beat on the window screaming that he needed a ride.

Bob said, "Show him the gun Sadie," as he jammed it into reverse and started backing up. Sadie pointed the shotgun and the man jumped down. She watched him drop to his knees and start to cry.

Bob backed it right up the on ramp hitting a little car with the back of the trailer and shoving it out of the way off to the side. He got it up on route 8 and headed north.

"We'll pick up 322 and go around that mess if we can get through Franklin." Bob muttered.

Sadie raised her hands in supplication not knowing where the heck they were. At least the trees were pretty, she thought as they picked their way along. They pulled over at a spot that looked deserted and Bob said, "Let's take a break, shall we? I got to piss like a horse."

Sadie was out the door, over the guardrail and behind a bush in no time. "No peeking!" she yelled.

Bob hollered back, "Don't worry I'm too busy to bother." After he zipped up he walked back to look at his trailer and was surprised when he saw no damage.

Sadie was standing by the fender when he came back. "It feels good to stretch my legs," she said.

"Yeppers," said Bob, "now let's take a few minutes. I could use some coffee and a bite, how 'bout you?"

"I don't see too many restaurants around here," Sadie said as she waved her arm.

"Ahh, madam will be pleased to know we have zee first class service aboard this yacht." Bob said with a horrible French accent.

They got back in and got in the sleeper. "Madam will be seated here." Bob gestured to one end of the bunk and sat down on the other as Sadie giggled.

"Your accent sucks," she said smiling

"Yeah well I try," he reached into a tiny closet and produced a coffee pot and a jug of water. "Here, plug this into the cigarette lighter and fill it with water while I see what's fir to eat."

There was a cooler that was plugged in also she noticed and Bob pulled lunchmeat, cheese, bread and mustard out of it. "It's like a little fridge," he said, "it can keep stuff warm too."

Then he reached over and pulled a fold up table down. "See, just like home," he smiled at her.

"I'm impressed," she nodded, "you got a Jacuzzi in here too?"

"Not yet, working on that one, I've seen some with little toilets and showers before but too small for me."

He was a big man, six two and about three hundred pounds she judged and he had the biggest hands she had ever seen.

They cleaned up the remnants of their meal and Bob said, "Well young lady, let's see what Franklin is all about."

After a scary crawl down the mountain leading into town they turned onto the main street and saw one place that had burnt but the town was in good shape. People were standing around in groups of two or three talking.

Bob stopped the truck when he saw a police officer standing by the curb. "Howdy Officer," he said, "have you heard any news, maybe know what's going on?"

"Not really, the power's out and nobody can get their cars to start. I see you're moving though," the officer noted. "Haven't heard anything either, phones, radios everythings kaput."

Bob told him everything he knew and saw that day. "Damn," said the cop, "all the way to Ohio? This must be one big ass snafu."

People started to gather around but Bob rolled his window up and drove off. He motored on in silence past stalled traffic and charred ruins. It was getting dark when suddenly he said, "Change of plans, we're going up to New York and get on 17, that will run us right to Binghamton. Sound good to you?"

"Yeah sure, I'm lost in space here." Sadie said with little emotion.

Bob was getting tired, very tired. He decided that after he got through Tionesta he would stop and sleep. He was at the bottom of the hill almost into town crossing the short bridge when there was a loud BANG!

The brakes locked up and the truck stalled. Sadie got tossed out of the bunk. "What the heck?" she mumbled.

"Oh shit," Bob swore, he restarted Maggie and pushed the airbrake release but nothing happened. "Damn." Bob got his flashlight and went out to look.

Millie Beachum lived in the first house off the bridge. She was eighty eight years old and half deaf but she heard that bang alright.

She kept her Lincoln continental parked right up by her porch even if she drove it once a month, maybe. Her yard was over grown, her house needed painting in the worst way.

She had 'POSTED,' 'NO TRESPASSING,' 'KEEP OUT,' 'NO FISHING OR HUNTING,' signs on every tree, post and side of her house.

She looked out her window at the big rig on the bridge. Her eyes narrowed and her lip curled up.

Damn trucks, she thought to herself, she told the town counsel to build another bridge over the river so the traffic wouldn't go past her house, but NOOOO, the state had to do that.

Then those idiots suggested she move if she didn't like the traffic. Those uppity assholes, she'd show them. She wouldn't ever vote again.

She slipped into her pink bunny slippers, put on her housecoat, Dolly Parton wig and snorkeling mask to keep the bugs out of her eyes and nose and went outside to tell that son of a gun he better move that damn truck or else!

Welcome to Tionesta, Bob and Sadie.

# CHAPTER SIXTEEN

October 17; The President of the United States of America welcomed the men and women gathered in the conference room.

"Today is an historic day, in this room and sheltered throughout this fine complex is the future of the world. In approximately ninety days we shall begin to take stock of what remains of the old order on the planet."

The secretary of the interior raised his hand like a grade school child. "I have a question Mr. President."

The President nodded to him to continue, "What about the nuclear reactors around the country and the world, won't they melt down and explode?"

The head of FEMA stood up and faced him. "We anticipated that and had agents in place to shut down the reactors two hours prior to the arrival of the CME." He then sat back down.

The President continued, "I was in conference with all the world leaders who mattered since the beginning of this sacred chance to rid the world of its weakest and most worthless population. All have agreed to come here and remain with us to safeguard their future."

The President looked around the room. "Projections show that the elderly, crippled, sick, mentally unbalanced and poor will be the first to perish. Leaving the others to fight among themselves.

By spring people, ninety percent of those leeches will be gone forever." There was spontainious applause.

General Porter was feeling a bit warm and had a tickle in his throat. He tried to ignore that as he concentrated on the good news the president was conveying.

". . . . and we will shred that archaic and liberal constitution and write a new order for our lives and for every living human of the newly united one world order. We will bulldoze away the old and build a bright and . . ."

General Porter sneezed and sneezed again. Sweat ran down his face as he fell out of his chair. He vomited and shat himself then sneezed again.

The great leaders of the nation and the would be new world looked aghast at the sick man and all bolted from the room. Five days later the great complex spread out underground across the country was a thirteen trillion dollar tomb.

# CHAPTER SEVENTEEN

Officer Coffey had to admit it, he hadn't been on a horse in a long time. Sheila, however still looked like the rodeo queen she once was.

"Which way?" he asked when they got back to the barracks.

Officer Smart was looking at the tarps covering the bodies lying in the dirt. "Hays, we'll go for Hays." She said and pulled on the reins.

They rode at a canter, Pat was starting to loosen up, get the feel for the animal again. They rode up to Waygo's little store but no one was there and the door was wide open.

Pat took a look around but didn't see anything amiss. He found a bucket and filled it with water to give the horses a drink.

"How's it feel to be a mounted lawman Pat?" Sheila asked, "not many left in Kansas anymore."

"There's Claude Johnson, he spends as much time on a horse as he does in a car." Pat looked up at her.

"Yeah, but there's only two roads in his whole district." she laughed. Just then both horses lifted their heads and pointed their ears towards the store. Horses can be better watchdogs than dogs at times.

Around the corner came Joe Waygo or what used to be Joe Waygo, he attacked. Sheila had her AR-15 laid across the saddle and quickly put two rounds in Joe's chest. He stumbled to his knees and fell flat on his belly.

Pat went back in the store again, this time with his shotgun and came out with a couple boxes of double ought buckshot.

"I left a quick note for Joe's wife. I figured she'd be more concerned about these than what happened to old Joe." He said.

"Mount up and ride cowboy," Sheila turned her horse and gave it a little kick.

Pat soon caught up, "I ain't used to this at all, I'm going to be mighty sore tomorrow. You however, look as comfortable as if you're sitting in a lawn chair at a bar-b-que."

"Well I ride all the time Pat, hell there are times I'd rather ride a horse than a cowboy."

"Yeah, just my luck." Said Pat

"You ever try your luck?" she said looking right at him.

He swallowed and kicked his horse.

Hays was swarming with zombies as they now called them. Their plan was simple, stay together, slay together.

They rode right down main street, the horses were a little skittish at first but soon got used to the gunfire and rampaging humans.

It was relatively easy, the infected came right at them but they had to shoot quick or ride away. Unlike all the classic zombie movies you did not have to shoot them in the head.

At the far end of town they found about ten dead ones outside a neat little brick house. Inside were Robin and Tyler Young both teenagers and their mom Lynn.

Tyler had a twenty two with a hundred round drum magazine on it. He simply pulled the trigger until they fell. Lynn guarded the back with an old sixteen gauge single barrel shotgun, there were four bodies on the ground out there.

"Mom had to shoot Dad, he was growling and tried to grab me." Robin, the thirteen year old called out the open window. She had a butcher knife duct taped to a broom handle. There was blood on it.

Sheila yelled down, "we'll be back to see you guys when we get a chance, don't let them near you."

Both officers were reloading. "Let's try and get in the hardware store, we're running low on ammo." Pat said.

There were some folks locked in rooms calling out the windows, a couple up on the roof top were waving and pointing in all directions. One lady was locked in her car and had screamed herself hoarse.

The early morning patrons of the Buffalo Gal saloon were locked inside and old Kelly was shooting out of the window with the old sawed off double barrel he kept under the bar. Sheila figured those patrons didn't mind being locked in.

There were six zombies coming towards them so they spurred their horses and rode up shooting. The hardware hadn't been opened yet when the whole thing started so Pat shot out the plate glass door and went inside.

Sheila held the reins to his gelding with one hand and was shooting her 9mm with her other.

"Hurry up Pat!" she called "there's more coming fast."

All of a sudden another rider on a magnificent black stallion burst from a side street, a pistol in each hand blazing away. Holding the reins in his teeth and guiding the horse with his knees. The rider, wearing a dirty white hat turned and Sheila saw it was Elmo Mc Murdy. He made one last shot and rode up to Officer Smart.

"I reckoned to get my money today but I see the courthouse is closed," he said as he reloaded his 45 caliber revolvers. "Good thing I brought Daddy's pistols with me just in case." He holstered one and started to reload the other.

Sheila was amazed, "Elmo, where did you learn to ride and shoot like that? That was . . . that was simply fantastic."

He blushed a little, "I read a lot of Louis La Mour books when I was a kid and practiced doing what he said those old cowboys did."

Sheila smiled as she shook her head, then made another shot. Pat came out with boxes of shells, he handed some to Sheila.

"Need bullets Elmo? They're free today. Pat nodded towards the store.

Elmo slipped out of the saddle and went in the store. "Mind you only grab shells Elmo." Pat called after him and then blasted an attacker with his twelve gauge. He didn't see the one finger salute Elmo gave him.

Townsfolk began to appear with guns and in a tight bunch they had the town cleared by four in the afternoon.

"I read about stuff like this in the history books," said Belle Raines, the widow who owned the drugstore, "never in my wildest dreams did I think I'd see something like I saw today. Are you a single man Mr. Mc Murdy?"

There's something about violence and near death that makes people horny.

Pat and Sheila were sitting outside the Buffalo Gal having a beer and cleaning their rifles, talking about forming an old fashioned posse and riding to the next town when an old 54 Chevy pickup drove down the street.

Lester Spotted Calf got out and looked around in total amazement. He walked over to the officers and said, "I came into town to find out why the power was still out. Did everybody get in an argument or something? I can see thirty bodies or so."

"No Lester," said Sheila, "this here is the result of a real life zombie apocalypse."

"Damn," he said, "all those conspiracy nuts were right."

"Hey Lester," Pat asked, "how'd you get that truck to start?"

"Huh? I just turned the key and mashed down on the starter switch, same as always. Why?"

"Well friend, you may have the only running vehicle in the county."

Lester smiled, "I do take care of it." They all looked at the truck with smoke rising from under the hood, a cracked windshield and dirt from 1962 still on it.

"I guess you do," said Pat as Bill Reedy walked up.

"Near as we can figure," Bill said, "there are two hundred and twenty seven dead here in town and over three hundred missing. Ben and Ida Best opened their store and are cooking up all the meat they can on that big gas grill they have, so if you're hungry go on over."

Evening was creeping in, they had people watching for more zombies. It was time to rest, it had been a long day.

Oh, and in case you're interested, Pat did get lucky that night.

# CHAPTER EIGHTEEN

Brad woke up and looked at the battery powered clock on the nightstand which was an old empty beer keg and a piece of plywood sitting on top.

6:30am, he was used to getting up then and wasn't surprised. What was surprising was how cold it was, he could see his breath. The fire musta went out.

He jumped out of bed, dressed in a hurry, put on his hat and coat and ran to the outhouse. Afterwards, fully awake now, he lit the cooking stove for some instant heat, put on some water for coffee and went to light the wood burner.

He had bought it two years ago after seeing a flyer at the Superduper. It was nice and big with glass doors so he could watch the fire.

Paper, kindling, and a match. Then a couple of bigger chunks of maple. In a short while it was nice and warm.

There was sparkling frost on everything outside including the cabins windows. Brrr.

He made a cup of instant and stood with his butt close to the fire. The sun was shining and by nine it was warming up. He was definitely cutting more wood today but first, he checked his wallet, he was going to go see Jake.

He decided to take his revolver in case he saw a bear and went outside. It was nice out, the frost had disappeared and the sky was a deep blue with no clouds. He thought he would walk.

As he neared the driveway to Jake's place he heard some shouting and stopped. Cautiously he edged up to the tree line by the road and could now see Jake's house.

He saw two men with their backs to him and in front of them stood Jake and Mary with their hands in the air. Jake was telling them they were welcome to his truck but it didn't run.

"Bullshit, we saw you driving it the other day. Now where's the damn keys?" one of them said.

"They're in it, go look." Jake said calmly.

Brad didn't hesitate, he pulled his gun, took a two handed stance and shouted, "DROP IT AND FREEZE OR I WILL SHOOT!"

He saw the pistol as the one on the right started to turn and Brad pulled the trigger. From a distance of thirty feet the 41 caliber slug hit the man in the chest just below the shoulder and threw him backwards. The gun fell out of his grip.

The other man immediately raised his arms and begged. "Please don't shoot me, I don't have a gun."

Jake picked up the fallen weapon and pointed it at the criminal. Mary walked up to him and punched him in the eye, knocking him down. "Get up scumbag," she said to him.

"Man, you picked the right time to show up with that hog leg." Jake said, "These assholes wanted to steal my truck, imagine that."

Brad kept pointing his gun at the man on the ground and advanced on him. He looked fairly dead.

Brad turned and looked at the other one. Dark blue coat, black woolen watch cap, dirty jeans. He was as skinny as a fat skeleton. Bloodshot eyes and rotten teeth, the dead guy looked better.

Jake spoke to him, "What did you think you were doing? What?"

"We, we wanted to leave but our car wouldn't start. Mook was tired of walking, it was all his idea, honest." The waste head said.

"Right," said Brad, "if he was up and you were down he'd say the same thing."

"No, no you don't understa . . ."

"Shut up, what were you doing up here?" Jake hollered at him.

"Nuttin, we was, uh, we was camping out, like the boy scouts." He stuttered.

Mary hauled back and punched him again. "You tell my husband the truth or I'll get my butcher knife and cut your peenie weenie dick off." She shouted at him.

Brad had never seen Mary angry before, she was nuts!

"We was, we was cooking bath salts and we got to get it to Pittsburgh." He said looking at the ground.

"Cover him Brad," Jake said, "if he moves, shoot him in the head." Jake handed Mary the gun he had and frisked the guy. He found a knife and a dope pipe.

"What do we do with him?" asked Brad.

"Let me shoot him." Mary said a little too quickly.

"Not yet honey buns, first give me back the gun and then go get the camera." Jake said holding out his hand.

She gave it to him and went in the house. They took a picture of the live dickhead and then a couple of the dead one. It was an old Polaroid and the pictures came out pretty good.

Jake then had Mary get a can of spray paint and outline the body on the grass. "Now Mr. dumb bunny you're gonna drag him over in the woods and dig a nice hole." Jake gestured with the gun. "Mary, get the shovel."

Over in the woods they found a brown duffel bag full of bags of powder. After the skinny shit dug a deep enough hole, he drug the body over and rolled it into the grave. Jake tossed the duffel in with it. "Fill it in." he commanded the prisoner.

"Now what do we do with him?" Brad asked Jake.

"Well, we can't call Wolfy to come get him so we'll have to take him into town. We'll tie him up and you can get your four wheeler and trailer. He and I can fit in it." Jake then turned to Mary but she was already holding a length of rope.

Brad took off. On the way back the enormity of what just happened hit him like a slap in the face. He started to tremble, then went to one knee.

After making deals with God that we don't really want to know about, he got up and took off at a determined pace.

The trailer was still hooked up and empty now. He filled the gas tank with the oil mix and put the half full can in the trailer and bungeed it down. It started on the second pull and emitted its customary cloud of smoke.

I bet those were the guys the Sheriff was looking for he thought as he eased the clutch out and maneuvered around his truck.

Mary punched the would be thief in the ear for old time's sake as he struggled to get in the trailer. He fell right in.

# CHAPTER NINETEEN

The bird flu was bad, entire communities left empty and silent. It skipped some people, one in every five hundred thousand or so.

San Diego was full of ghosts. In a quiet little house on thirty third street Gary Bond sat in his kitchen. He was thinking about how unfair it all was. A sixty five year old college professor of arts and antiquities, he was truly upset.

Now that the whole world had gotten sick and died just after the power went off and it was stinking outside with dogs running in packs. He would never get to retire, move to San Salvador and search for the Mayan city he had good reason to know where to look for so he could claim discovery and write the book that would crown his career.

Being gay, he lived alone in the same house he had been born in. His mother had been a widow who had lost her husband she had only spent two days of wedded bliss with on the island of Tarawa.

Alone at home when the labor pains began, she tried to get to the telephone but the pains were so intense she laid down by the front door. The baby came quickly like it couldn't wait to see the world.

The mail man had heard the baby crying and knowing Mrs. Bond was very pregnant, knocked on the door and asked if she was all right.

After an ambulance ride to the hospital both were kept for two days and then pronounced fit to go home.

Gary grew up in the fifties, a very good time to grow up, almost an age of innocence. His mother noticed he would rather play tea party with girls than play baseball and thought that at least he wouldn't be getting hurt on the diamond.

Gary was a handsome young man even though he never grew taller that five foot one inch. He was very smart and could play the piano. At college he met Lincoln and they became very good friends.

Gary and Linc got involved in the gay movement sweeping through California and marched at the front of every parade. Then the AIDS virus came along and took Linc away from him.

His career, as he thought of it as a futile effort to educate the "X" generation, the "me" generation, the whatever generation had merely been a means of expanding his knowledge of his doctrinaire work on the Mayan civilization.

Wasted, all those years of patience, the countless hours of research, to be thrown away by another rogue disease.

He had to leave the city. The decomposing bodies would create more sickness and the dogs might want some fresh meat.

He carried clothes and supplies out to the attached garage where the 1962 Ford Falcon he inherited from his mother was kept. It was in very good shape, having been well cared for over the years.

Only one block to the campus, two blocks to the grocery store and a few short trips to the beach, (Gary liked to look at young men) was all it was ever driven. He made it a point to keep the gas tank full.

Finally, loaded up with his belongings and the framed wedding picture of his mother and father he opened the garage door and heard crying.

It was a child crying. It came from the neighbor's backyard. Gary took three steps and looked over the fence.

There was a filthy little girl of about three years of age sitting in the dirt with tears running, creating a mud film on her face. She looked up and said, "Who're you?"

Gary stared at her for a few seconds and replied, "I'm your grandfather you haven't met and I'm here to get you."

Gary hurried around to the neighbor's driveway but the heavy gate was locked. The front door was locked as well. Gary picked up a chair on the front porch and broke the window beside the door. He carefully reached in and unlocked it.

Inside, a dead woman lay stinking on the couch. He kept on to the open backdoor and went in the backyard and took the child in his arms.

"You poor dear, all alone." He said to her.

The little girl, clad only in wet shorts smeared her tear streaked face and said, "Mommy sick." Gary began to cry.

He took her upstairs to the bathroom being careful not to let her see the dead woman. He bailed water out of the toilet tank and washed her, found her some clean clothes and packed some more for her. In a short time they were driving away east out of the city.

While the baby was sitting on the front seat eating seedless grapes and making quite a mess he noted, Gary began to think.

I don't know anything about small children, what am I doing? He carefully steered around a motionless bread truck and looked at her. He realized that she, like himself was a rare commodity now. A living, breathing, healthy, human being.

Gary pulled into the parking lot of a grocery store. Carrying the child, he walked in through the broken doors. It had been looted but there was still plenty of stuff.

Grabbing a cart he put her in the little seat facing him and went shopping. Children's juice containers, bags of lollypops, little animal crackers, lots of that stuff was still there.

Oh, and his favorite, canned sardines in mustard sauce and oh! There is a God! Pickled herring.

He came out with the cart full of bagged goodies, (he had been a bag boy in the ancient past) and filled the back seat.

All through that day's journey he saw death, destruction, emptiness and the remains of chaos. The little girl . . . . He didn't know her name! Why hadn't he asked her, her name? had gone to sleep.

He drove on in silence. His father's parents had a place out by the Salton Sea. It was his now as they were long dead and he the only heir.

They arrived by evening and Gary found the battery powered lamp. He fed the child and learned her name was Sasha, he read her the book Animal House as it was the closest thing he had to a children's book.

He then dressed her for bed in one of his pastel sweatshirts. As he tucked her in she looked at him with trusting innocence in her eyes and said, "nite, nite, 'amppa."

Gary wept again.

# CHAPTER TWENTY

Sheriff Wolfgang J Culpepper was still out on the streets, peddling his wife's bicycle. He was checking locks and reassuring folks that everything was going to be okay.

He had his powerful eight cell flashlight taped to the basket of his wife's antique pink Schwinn. They had been pretty lucky when the power went out, only the newspaper building caught fire and by a miracle the neighboring places hadn't burnt. Though the funeral home next door was a little brown on one side.

He was on the south side of town when he heard the truck coming and then the explosion. It was an old one speed bike and his legs were tired but he went to investigate.

He arrived just in time to hear old Millie yell, "This ain't no parking lot! Get that damn thing outta here!"

There was a flashlight shining out from under the drive axles and a pair of legs sticking out. The man scooted out from under and shown his light at the lady and said, "What the fah . . ." He was looking at a four foot tall creature wearing fluffy pink bunnies with twenty five miles of curly blonde hair and a snorkeling mask with the orange breather tube waving in the air.

Oh God, he thought, I'm hallucinating.

There was another light shining on at him and a man's voice called out from behind it. "Now calm down Miss Millie, you shouldn't be out here, it's getting cold. Now let me handle this."

"Just get him out of here or by God I'll vote you out of office!" she shouted as she turned and stomped off in a huff.

The flashlight bobbed around a bit then went still and a man in a police uniform sans hat stepped into the light. He was a slight man with sharply creased trousers and not a hair out of place. He smiled as he said, "Sheriff Culpepper here, what seems to be the problem?"

"Well Sheriff, I'd like to move it like the nice lady suggested but the old girl blew a pancake gasket and the brakes are locked up." Bob said as evenly as he could.

"Oh," Wolfy said, not having any idea what a pancake gasket was, "you got your license on you?" Bob handed it over.

"Hmmm, Robert Prince, Slippery Rock, where you going Bob?" the officer asked, tilting his light to shine on Bob's face.

"New York, then New Jersey. I-80 is a mess and I thought I'd pick up route 17 and go across that way." Bob said watching his license in the cop's hand.

"That makes sense." Wolfy said handing the laminated card back. Bob gave a little sigh of relief because the longer a cop held on to your license the more trouble you were in.

Sadie was dumbfounded, first, this tiny lady all dressed up for Halloween appears and starts yelling her head off at Bob. Then a cop arrives on a pink ladies bike.

This is one weird place she thought as she rubbed her head. She had bumped it on the doorsill of the sleeper when the brakes locked up but nothing was broken. Sore, but not broke.

Bob climbed back in and shut Maggie down. "Come on, he's gonna show us where the motel is. There's nothing we can do right now."

Bob told the Sheriff everything he had told the cop in Franklin as they walked along. "Wow," said Wolfy, "you've had quite a day, so, no power clear past Akron huh? Nothing running but your truck and you're not sure why. Looks like a mighty big pickle to me." Wolfy set the bicycle on its stand so the light shown on the office door of the motel and knocked.

A nice looking matron opened it up. 'evening Sarah," Wolfy said, "I brought you some business. Got a couple of truckers that broke down."

"I got one room left and it's a double." She sniffed looking at Bob and Sadie, "she your wife or your daughter?" indicating Sadie. "Daughter," Bob answered immediately.

"Well, okay," she pulled the door open wide, "seeing how Wolfy brought you. He knows I don't 'low no funny business here."

Wolfy coughed, knowing full well that Sarah and Racine her partner were lesbians and did all kinds of funny business themselves. "Just give them the room Sarah, he looks awful tired."

She harrumphed and started to write on a form, "Credit card reader is down. Do you have cash?"

Bob pulled out his wallet and opened it, "how much?" he was getting grumpy.

"Forty nine, forty eight sir, for the double. Check out is promptly at eleven."

What a prissy bitch, Sadie thought, and what's up with the butch hair cut? She didn't know it but Sarah and Racine were known around town as "Butch and Bud."

"Sign here please," and she turned the form, handed Bob the pen and his ID while she snatched the fifty he was holding.

"Keep the change," Bob muttered. He had to lie down, soon.

"Here," said Sarah and handed him two candles, "on the house. Be careful you don't set the place on fire." Bob held up his flashlight and pushed them back.

It was chilly in the room but there were spare blankets in the closet. Bob toed his boots off, slipped beneath the covers and was soon asleep.

Sadie sat up a little while thinking of all the crazy events of the last three days that had got her to where she was sharing a motel room with a man older than enough to be her father. At least there were separate beds.

Sheriff Culpepper pedaled for home. It had been quite a day. It started off with talking with the mayor about Halloween trick or treat time to what might be a regional disaster or worse.

He had to help push a couple of cars off the road, helped to put out three fires and got soaked in the rain walking home to get the bike. He had seen the night deputy walking to the office earlier so he didn't bother stopping in there. From the looks of things there wasn't going to be any calls anyway.

His wife had sandwiches ready and got him a cold beer after he sat down. He wasn't used to all the physical exercise and was soon in bed and sound asleep.

# CHAPTER TWENTY ONE

Everyone was up early at the Swende house. Sam was stoking the wood burner, the kids were all looking out the window at the frost, Goofy was nudging hands wanting petted.

Becca came down, put on her coat and went outside to fill a bucket to flush the toilet. Having the power out wasn't a rare thing where they lived and they coped with the little problems without a fuss. There were bigger fish to catch.

Arnie and Sam siphoned all the gas out of the tractor and poured it in the truck. They were going to take the orphans into town and see what the authorities wanted to do.

Mattie went up to get Sally who was sitting quietly with Clay, Jimmy had joined them as well. "Well," she said, "you guys ready for a ride into town?"

All three children turned their heads at the same time and in unison said, "No, we need to stay here."

Mattie was taken aback. "But the men put gas in the truck wouldn't it be fun to ride in the back to town?"

"Yes Mrs. Swende," Sally spoke up, "it would be fun but we know we must stay here."

"What do you mean, you know?"

Jimmy spoke up, "Just like we know that my grandparents are dead, like Sally's mom and Gus."

Mattie almost stumbled and fell. "Nobody knows that for sure, has Sam been talking to you?"

"Mom, we just know. Okay?" Clay said matter of factly.

Mattie stared at the three children and said, "Wait here." She wasted no time getting down the stairs. "Becca!" Mattie was starting to freak out, "Did anyone tell the kids about their families?"

"I don't think so, Sam and Arnie wanted to wait until they had talked to Wolfy."

"Those kids KNOW, how, I can't explain but they just told me they knew."

"Let me get Sam," Becca said and went out the front. Mattie put her hands to her temples and whispered to herself, "Oh God, oh my God."

When the men rushed in with Becca all three children were standing on the stairs.

Clay spoke first, "Mom, Dad, what we said is true isn't it?"

Jimmy said, "Sam and Mr. Swende must go into town but it is best if we, including Barry and Terry stay here." The twins walked into the room from the outside.

Now it was Sally's turn, "We don't know why we know but we do. We also know the whole world is dying right now. We see this through other kid's eyes, all of us are now united."

There was stunned silence. Clay spoke, "The ones who left us to our fate are now dying, they will not see the light of day again."

Jimmy spoke up, "There are three men coming, there has been blood."

Then finally Sally, "It is safe for us here, we must stay until the others come." At that the three turned and went back up the stairs. Terry and Barry followed them.

Arnie looked at Mattie, who looked at Becca, who looked at Sam. Goofy started barking, there was a noise outside. It was somebody on a four wheeler with Jake and somebody else in a little trailer.

"Hello the house, anyone home?" Jake called out.

Sam said, "Don't say a word." Jake walked up to the door just as Arnie opened it.

"Jake, it's good to see you, who'er these guys?"

"The good looking fella on the machine is Brad, he's a good guy. Mr. dickhead asshole in the trailer is not. Him and a partner tried to steal me and Mary's truck this morning and probably would have killed us. Brad showed up at the right time and stopped them."

"Well, where's the other guy?" asked Arnie.

"Oh, Brad there," Brad waved, "shot his heart out and saved our lives, that punk ass surrendered." Jake said nodding his head.

Arnie looked at Sam who asked, "Is Mary okay?"

"Yeah, pissed off but just fine." Jake said. Brad had kept quiet, he didn't know anyone but he trusted Jake.

He finally spoke up, "We're taking this one to see Wolfy, I mean the Sheriff."

Arnie chuckled a little, "We were just headed down that way, you think you can keep that desperado in the bed of Sam's truck?"

The four men and a prisoner left in the truck, the children all watched them go from the upstairs windows. The gamma rays affected all the children in the world between the ages of three and puberty. They became one, united from a release of part of the brain that had been blocked throughout the ages, sort of a common bond.

Like the Borg on Star Trek, like ants in a more understandable way. A collective mind as a certain professor in California would later call it.

What one child saw, they all saw. By the second day of the worldwide blackout they were all connected to a common path. Their bond was solid, their bond was liquid, their bond saved many lives.

But I'm getting ahead of the true story and I'm sure you want all the details. Like we all wanted to watch the final seconds of John F Kennedy's life, then were sorry we saw the film.

The men came down off of German Hill road and made the turn on main street. The Sheriff's office was just past the courthouse that hadn't seen a trial in years.

"Look at that," said Jake, as they drove past the burned out county paper.

"Just my luck," said Sam, "we just paid a years subscription."

"Imagine the story they could write today." Brad said. They didn't see the patrol Jeep but stopped at the office anyway.

Deputy Leroy "DAWG" Lewiston was at the desk. He didn't know where Wolfy was, he didn't know where Chrissy the dispatcher was, he didn't know nothing except there wasn't any doughnuts this morning and that pissed him off.

6' 6" and 422 pounds he really liked his doughnuts. He looked like a pear shaped bear in a uniform and his shaved head didn't help with the ladies even though he thought it was sexy.

His daddy was the ousted mayor who was shacking up with some drunk woman in Titusville. He liked being called "DAWG" as he thought it made him sound tough, he made no connection with the cartoon.

He was a smart enough fella to do his paperwork right and to avoid Wolfy whenever he could. He liked intimidating the campers every summer but soon it would be winter and the only person he impressed then was Sassy Vanwormer, the very large woman who lived across the river.

It was okay though as she didn't ask for much and gave good head.

He watched as a skinny little man with his hands tied behind his back was shoved through the door.

"Help me," he said, "these sons'a bitches kilt my friend and are gonna kill me if you don't stop them."

Now Leroy ain't a bad person, he was raised in the Methodist faith, he knew right from wrong but when he saw Jake in the entourage he had his doubts.

For years he and Jake had been playing cat and mouse over Jake growing a little weed here and there. Actually Jake grew about twenty two hundred pounds a year from his indoor stuff to the three thousand acres he used courtesy of the federal government.

Well, hey, that was just the way the ball bounced. It made sense and money. Nobody knew that Jake and Mary had a daughter who had been, "physically and mentally challenged" as the doctor had put it. Jake paid cash for the best care she could have.

"Lock him Dawg, that's the last surviving member of the bath salts cooking and car thievery corporation," Sam thundered, "and don't listen to his snarky little lies either."

Dawg was tired, his car wouldn't start and he had, had to walk the three blocks to work, he hadn't had any coffee and there wasn't any Goddamned doughnuts.

They had one cell in the back and to lock him up meant that he would have to get up and walk back there to do it. He knew Sam of course, as well as the other four hundred and some odd people who lived in and around Tionesta all year long.

He knew Wolfy would be pissed if he didn't do something.

He heaved himself up out of the chair and grabbed the metal ring with the one big key on it and said with a sigh, "Bring him back here."

# CHAPTER TWENTY TWO

Wolfy glided the Schwinn into the parking area of his office. Sam's truck was there and he could see the place was crowded, it looked like another interesting day. He saw Brad Singer look at him as he toed down the kickstand.

"Hey, Wolfy's here," Brad told the others. Dawg heard that as he was locking the cell door and was relieved. Not his problem anymore.

The Sheriff walked in and Jake told him the whole story, showed him the three pictures he had and praised Brad for saving his life. Wolfy didn't say a word, taking the pictures with him as he squeezed past his deputy he went back to the cell.

"Is what I just heard true? This is your one and only chance to help yourself." The veteran law man said sternly to the frightened, skinny man.

"I want a lawyer." He said.

"That's it, you're done for now." Wolfy said and began to read him the Miranda rights. "Wait, wait! Will it really help me?" the burned out coward let his voice fall.

"Yes son," the Sheriff said in a kindly way, "I'll personally tell the judge that you co-operated and he'll weigh that in when he makes his decision."

Wolfy listened and heard pretty much the same story. He told the man he had done the right thing and walked back out to the desk.

Everybody had sat down now except Brad who was pretty nervous, besides there weren't any more chairs.

Wolfy walked in, "I'll have to get everybody's statement, I have a battery powered tape recorder here somewhere but it looks as if you're free to go Mr. Singer. That was a clear case of justifiable homicide. The DA will want to talk to you after this electric problem is fixed so don't leave the country. I'll keep you notified." Brad wiped a little bead of sweat off his forehead. "Dawg, where's the paperwork?"

"I uh, uh, didn't get to it yet. They had just got here before you came in." Dawg said holding his hands up in a what'er gonna do manner.

"You locked a man in my cell without charging him or booking him?" Wolfy was incredulous. He lowered his voice and leaned in. "You idiot, he could be set free for that," Wolfy was shaking mad, "you get your fat ass back there and read him his rights and do the damn paperwork. Jesus frying clams!"

He turned and faced the others and asked Sam and Arnie if they had witnessed any of the crime.

"No," said Arnie, "Jake and Brad stopped at the house and we gave them a ride down here."

"Oh," said the Sheriff who then looked up, "did you say a ride?"

"Yeah, Sam's truck." Wolfy went and looked out the window.

"Geez Wolfy," Sam exclaimed, "you parked that spiffy little bike right beside it, you gonna go whole hog and put some streamers on the hand grips? Ha, maybe paint it black and white and get a flashing light from the hardware store. I see you already installed a spot light."

Everybody started laughing except Dawg who was staring at a piece of paper and chewing on a pen. He never heard them.

Wolfy told them about the semi and Miss Millie and everything the trucker had told him. Brad then remembered what he had heard on the radio and added that bit of information too.

"Planet wide?" Wolfy shook his head in wonder, "It could be a year or more before the juice starts flowing again."

"Ahh, Wolfy?" Arnie spoke up, "There's another matter too." He told about Sam seeing the charred bodies and the four kids at his house. He didn't mention their odd behavior though.

"When it rains, it pours,' Wolfy muttered as he was writing on his notepad, "Sam, you have got a new job as deputy taxi driver. Raise your right hand."

Sam became a deputy. "Uh Sheriff, what are we going to do about gas?" Sam asked as he stuck himself with the badge's pin, ow.

Sam and the Sheriff drove over to the convenience store which just so happened to be open and lit up. The owner had wisely invested in a generator and by sheer luck had it stored in a metal shed. The gas problem was solved at the counties expense.

Wolfy then had Sam drive him down to the funeral home where the director was also the county coroner.

The three men squeezed in on the GMC's bench seat and stopped back at the office for the others. They dropped Arnie off at his place and Brad followed them back to Jake's place on the atv.

They dug up the body and removed the bag containing the dope. "Nice shot," said the coroner, "the bullet destroyed the heart muscle."

They put the dead guy in one of the body bags they had brought along and loaded it in the trucks bed. Jake and Brad stayed there and the other men left for more grisly business.

They went from burned out house to burnt out house and soon ran out of body bags. Tired and covered in ash and soot they drove back to the funeral home and unloaded the fruits of their search.

"We're going to have to bury these bodies as soon as we can because the cooler is down and there really isn't space in there anyway. I'll conduct an autopsy on the shooting victim of course. It is, in my opinion that everyone else died by accident. Do you agree, Sheriff?"

Wolfy nodded, he didn't know if he could speak just yet or not.

"I only have three caskets, I'll have to go see the Amish and have them build some more." The coroner, who also played the organ at the Methodist Church grimly said.

Sam and Wolfy drove back to the Quick Stop, refilled the tank and Wolfy sprung for sodas and sandwiches. Neither man was in the mood for conversation and sat there in the truck eating quietly.

"Points," Sam spoke up finally, "points is why I think this old girl is still running. Something happened that ruined the electronics in all the other newer cars. What we need to do is look around and see if there are any more old cars and trucks that still run."

Wolfy nodded and pulled out his notepad and pen for what seemed the hundredth time that day. "We got to have a town meeting and ask everybody. That would be the best way to find out. We'll drive around and tell everyone we see and ask them to spread the word. As fast as nasty rumors fly around this town it shouldn't take too long before everybody knows about it. We can all meet in the Presbyterian Church, better tell the Mayor first. She can set the time."

Sam nodded and let out a sigh, it was going to be a long day.

# CHAPTER TWENTY THREE

Bob woke up and laid there for a minute, then mother nature called. He pulled back the covers and swung his legs out. Still in his clothes he went to the bathroom.

Sadie awoke when the door clicked shut. Then she heard Bob groaning, it was cold in here she thought, they would have been better off in the truck.

The toilet flushed and Bob came out scratching his head leaving the door open. As he was putting on his boots Sadie sat up and said, "Oh my God, what is that awful smell?" she looked at Bob, "Tell me that didn't come out of you, arrrgh."

"Guilty as charged, I'm afraid," Bob's face turned red, "didn't have any matches, sorry."

Sadie moaned and pulled the blankets up over her head. "What are you going to do about Maggie?" The muffled voice under the motel comforter asked.

"I have a plan, how are you at turning wrenches?"

The blankets swooshed back over and Sadie said, "No luck there I'm sure, I don't know a ratchet from a monkey wrench."

"Well, do you think you can keep that crazy old lady at bay while I work underneath?"

"I can try Bob, I can only try." Then it was Sadie's turn at the bathroom.

Bob put on his hat and coat and walked over to the motel office. He told the lady at the desk they were checking out and asked if there was a big parking lot in town.

"Yes Sir," said Racine who was wearing a flannel shirt and had a Pirates baseball cap on her head, "three or four blocks down on the left is the Superduper. If that doesn't suit you there's one at the end of town by the Dollar Store."

Bob thanked her and walked back to the room but Sadie was coming out. "I hope you got everything, the toilet won't flush now."

"Yeah, let's go, you can make coffee if you would please in the truck, while I dig out my tools and overalls."

They walked back to where Maggie waited past the burnt out newspaper building and quiet houses that showed a few faces looking out at them past the curtains.

"You said the brakes were locked up, can you fix that?" Sadie asked.

"Can't really fix it until I get a new gasket, might need the whole can but I can back the brake shoes off and make it so we can move it." Bob said matter of factly. "It just won't have any brakes."

He unlocked the doors as Sadie crawled in to find the coffee pot then started the motor to let it warm up and charge the batteries. Back outside he opened a side box and removed a one piece jump suit that he donned and pulled out his toolbox.

"Coffee's hot," Sadie told him as he climbed back in. He gratefully took the cup she offered, blew on it and looked out the windshield. He saw an old pickup with three or four men in the back turn onto the main street and drive off.

He had a second cup that he took with him so he could get down to business. The sun had come out and it was a glorious cloud free day without any jet trails. It was warming up fast.

It was chilly in Millie's house though as she sat drinking a glass of juice. She heard the truck start up and thought about those damn dirty fumes it was putting out.

She put on her galoshes, faux sable fur coat and a maroon Russian flap cap and went out the door. This took a little while as she couldn't decide if she needed a scarf or not.

Sadie saw her coming and exited the warm cab. Millie marched up to where Bob's boots were sticking out and said, "Will you shut that damn thing off? You're polluting my air with this noisy damn thing."

"I'm busy lady, trying to move it so . . ."

"Don't you talk back to me, you damn dirty truck driver. I know all about your kind, with your damn dirty whores and your . . . ."

"HEY! You crazy old Bitch," Sadie was upset, "this is the kindest, nicest man I ever met. He saved me when I was at my worst, if it wasn't for him I'd be giving two dollar blow jobs just to eat. So SHUT UP and leave him alone."

Millie was shocked, nobody ever talked that way around her much less TO her. Millie owned thirty seven oil leases in the area, several rental properties, two coal mines and the Big Banana soft serve. She was, after all the richest person in town.

Bob of course, heard all that and swiveled his butt and sat up. He looked at the two women.

"Nice man is he?" Millie sniffed.

"Yes ma'am, a very nice man." Sadie said, a lot calmer now.

"I see, just be sure and move it." And with that Millie turned and walked off.

Bob shook his head and said quietly, "wow." Thirty minutes later Bob had adjusted each drum and was ready to try it. He eased the clutch up in first gear and the big rig moved ahead cautiously.

Bob shifted up to third and switched his jake brake on. "It'll be noisy but it will slow us tight down," he told Sadie.

He saw the entrance for the grocery store, slowed it with the jake, dropped it into second and turned in. he pulled up by the car wash, left in gear and used the jake to stall it and bring it to a stop.

They looked around, there was the Superduper, lit up and open. The post office, closed, a dinor, closed, and to Bob's relief a pharmacy.

"Home, sweet home," he said to Sadie. They went in the grocery.

Wade Kizsrinkski was worried. The manager and part owner of the Superduper was using his generator but it was old and began to make a funny noise soon after he got it running. He had plenty of stock but if the freezers went out there would be a major loss.

His cashier and deli girl showed up for work, they could walk in but his meat cutter lived out of town. Oh well, he thought, I've sliced pork chops before.

The Mayor walked in with a smile, "Hello Wade," she said brightly, "I see you're open and ready for business."

Mayor Helen Stroup was a gracious lady, always well groomed and dressed. Polite and attentive, she was in her third term. A bit on the perky side, she conducted town business with a sharp, clear mind. She was no pushover.

Her husband Joe ran the VFW and together they owned the laundry mat.

"Good morning Mrs. Mayor, how are you today?" Wade and Helen had, had a brief and very discreet affair several years ago but were still close friends.

Wade noticed a big man wearing a cowboy hat and a young woman had walked in and got a cart.

"Call me Helen, you old fool," she laughed, "anyway I just wanted to touch base with you and tell you we haven't heard a word from anybody about how long the power will be out or when someone can fix all the cars."

"Well . . . Helen, we'll stay open for normal business hours or until the generator dies, whichever happens first."

"I will count on you," she said, her eyes smiling, "you were always so . . . resourceful. Ta ta."

He watched her hips sway as she walked away and started thinking about when they had . . . "Mr. K I need ones." Heather the cashier, interrupted his thoughts.

# CHAPTER TWENTY FOUR

The baby was pushing on his arm, "ake up, ake up, Gary." He woke up. "ady coming today." Sasha was looking at him.

"That's nice, now watch out Grandpa has to go to the bathroom." Gray threw the covers back and got up. Clad in his boxers and T shirt he made his way in past the door and shut it.

He looked in the commode and discovered the child had already been there. He took some toilet paper and wiped the seat clean. At least she's potty trained, he mused.

As he sat there he thought, Gary? He didn't remember telling the little girl his name, only grandpa. What lady? He flushed the toilet and noticed it didn't fill back up.

Now he wanted his tea, there wasn't any water in the spigot. He went out and looked in the car, one liter of bottled water. He would have to get some.

He went back in and remembered he had an electric stove. Perplexed, he gave the baby a carton of apple juice and some sugar puffs in a bowl, no milk. The child was watching him.

He got the tea kettle and poured half the water in it. Now, he had to heat it. How? Outside on the patio there was a big brick grill.

He'd start a fire like the Indians did. He took some paper and stuffed it in the charcoal pit. Matches, where were some matches?

He found some charcoal, a big can of lighter fluid. No matches. He dumped the charcoal on top of the paper. He sprayed a liberal amount of fluid on it.

Gary was clever, there was a cigarette lighter in the dash of the car. Still in his boxers, Sasha watched from the window. Her bowl of cereal held to her side, sugar puffs stuck to her fingers.

Gary held an envelope and applied it to the red hot lighter. It smoldered but would not ignite. He blew gently on it, there! Fire! He shielded the fragile flame as he went back to the grill. He bent over and watched closely as he pushed the flame in. BLAM!! The lighter fluid lit.

Gary, his face red, like he was blushing and minus eyebrows. Placed the kettle on the middle of the grill.

Sasha was laughing with sugar puffs stuck to her chin. Gary saw the toddler in the window and smiled and waved. She aped that right back at him.

The water whistled, Gary grabbed the handle, burned his hand and dropped the kettle getting some boiling water on his bare leg.

Finally, he was able to sit down with half a cup. Sasha had found a pen and was busy doing artwork on Gary's white leather couch.

Gary opened a box of ho ho's and Sasha wanted two and promptly smeared them all over her face and hands while eating them. Breakfast over, professor Bond got dressed.

The next two hours was a valuable lesson on why you don't give children sugar unless they are someone else's problem.

Gary was tired, there were feathers in his hair from the pillow Sasha had hit him with, his hand was burnt, his eyebrows singed. There was a stain of unknown origin on his kacki shorts and the child was crying.

"Is there anyone in the house?" a voice from outside called out.

"Ady here," Sasha quit crying and pointed at the door.

Gary opened the door. A pretty young black woman dressed in shorts and halter top stood there. "Oh YES, I wasn't sure but there you are. Oh my, you're the first animated person I've seen in days, oh thank God."

"Uh, what do you . . ." Sasha pushed by Gary's legs touching the scalded place. "Ady, Ady," and ran into her arms.

"Oh my goodness, aren't we the messy one." The woman said and sasha began to giggle.

"Now wait a minute," said Gary, who was rubbing his leg. "who are you? And please put the child down."

"Believe it or not my name is Addie, for Adeline. I smelt the smoke and came to investigate, I'm glad I did."

"But, but . . ."

"Addie is my new mommy, ammpa," Sasha said and both adults looked at her. She had a big grin on her face.

Gary invited the young lady in and over a couple cans of warm cherry cola they talked. Addie was an army nurse but as there wasn't anyone to nurse anymore she left Fort Yuma and had been making her way west.

"I don't know why I stopped here but I did, then I found you two." Addie said with a shrug.

Gary was thinking, had Sasha known she was coming? Yes, she had said that first thing this morning. The business of knowing his name, (he was positive he hadn't told her), practically knowing Addie's name, impossible.

"It appears you have been adopted by a very precocious child." Gary told her.

"You know, that's okay by me, I mean what else could I do?" Addie leaned in and lowered her voice, "Professor, it would appear that you may need a little help here," she leaned back smiling.

He sighed and nodded. Three hours later Gary was smiling big time, Addie was a FIND! Not only was she at ease with Sasha, the child listened to her. She had Gary drive to a store where they found plenty of bottled water, canned goods, a propane camp stove, wooden matches, toys for Sasha, and a whole jar of pickled pigs feet for Gary.

She got a hose and a can and siphoned gas from a school bus. Gary was smart and stayed out of the way.

By evening they were eating a hot, nutritious meal by candle light. She had put ointment on Gary's scald and managed to bathe Sasha.

Sasha was sitting, holding a raggity ann doll and staring off into space. She stood up and came over to Gary and Addie.

"We must go to Aunt Lewis's Bizbo, meet Ollie." And with that she put herself to bed.

Gary said, "Aunt Lewis? Who's that?"

"I think she means San Luis Obispo." Addie said.

Gary told her of his experiences and suspicions with the little girl.

"Well Professor, if you are correct then we should go, to San Luis Obispo, hey, that rhymed!"

# CHAPTER TWENTY FIVE

Pat and Sheila led the posse consisting of twelve more men and women, including newly deputized Elmo McMurdy. The youngest member being Tyler Young, whom we met in a previous chapter. The oldest at seventy seven, Bill Langtry retired from the Double Diamond ranch was now riding shotgun for Lester Spotted Calf. Lester's truck became the supply center and chuck wagon.

They learned the zombies didn't attack horses or dogs but liked to bite cows and people of course.

The town of Learned was nothing but zees, they did find a mother and two children who were hiding in a tornado shelter but that was it.

Restocking their ammo and food supplies they pondered their next move. They began to call themselves the Kansas Rangers.

Bill Langtry thought it was appropriate that the cowboys and Indians were teamed up in this war.

Elmo was proving himself fearless and a skilled gunman. At one point riding right into a cluster of biting creatures, holding his reins in his teeth and making every shot count.

They lost Bill Reedy however, bitten he turned his gun on himself.

Fighting zombies from horseback proved to be the easiest way to do it, you just shot down into their heads. They couldn't do anything about the dead bodies and when finished they left them lay for the scavengers and camped out on the open grasslands.

They had added a U-haul trailer to the back of the truck and could now bring along more stuff.

They didn't know about the asian bird flu even though it had decimated Denver, the front range and spread into the mountains as well as north and south. For some reason it spared eastern Colorado, western Kansas and parts of Oklahoma.

It skipped a part of northern Alabama, some pockets of the Appalachians in West Virginia and Pennsylvania. There were isolated pockets scattered around the globe and each one had its own unique story but we won't get into that here.

The zombies, however were a regional problem. Pat and Sheila did think it odd that there hadn't been any government response at all. None, nada, no national guard, no FEMA, nothing.

Elmo said, (he was now included in the war counsel, he had earned the right) that they were either hiding in a hole or hanging from lampposts. Sheila thought that was about right and said if they could prove all this was the government's fault she'd help string 'em up.

Two days later they were looking at Wichita. Their band had grown to eighty some odd people, a couple hundred horses in the remuda. There was a 1960 Chrysler Imperial, two farm tractors with hay wagons and some feller riding a moped that smoked like a pipe.

Pat was looking through a pair of binoculars, "Wow," he said, "there must be thousands of them."

Sheila took the glasses and saw a swarming mass of bodies behaving like a gathering of gnats. "We might have to bypass this one." she spoke uncertainly, "we don't have enough bullets."

Lester Spotted Calf was standing there, "I know how to do it, we take a page from Crazy Horse."

Pat turned to him and said, "What do you mean Lester? This ain't the Little Big Horn."

"Nope, the Fetterman Massacre," he stated, "there's a huge gulley only a mile north of town where they used to mine limestone. Some of us play bait and every one slap jack of them will follow us in there, fish in a barrel."

"Lester, you just heard Officer Smart say we didn't have enough bullets." Pat was looking at him.

"No, but there are plenty of big round bales of hay all over the place we can light on fire and roll right down on them, burning them up." They pulled back and began to set the trap.

Actually it wasn't Crazy Horse's plan, he was one of the bait decoys. Red Cloud hatched the brilliant plot.

December 21st, 1866 was a bitterly cold day and they needed firewood at Fort Phil Kearny. A work detail left and had to go a mile from the fort to cut the wood.

Crazy Horse and nine warriors attacked the work party. This was clearly visible from the fort.

Captain Fetterman roused eighty one soldiers and two scouts to rescue them. The Indians rode a little ways off and began insulting the troops.

Fetterman then made his fatal mistake, he pursued the Indians to teach them a lesson. The decoys led them on, at times letting them catch up, most of the command were on foot. They would scrape ice from the ponies hooves, start small fires to warm their hands and when the army caught up would calmly remount and ride on infuriating Fetterman.

They were led into a deep depression where Red Cloud and about two hundred braves lay hidden in the rocks above. They didn't have a chance.

It took two days to set the trap. They didn't have to conceal anything so it was fairly easy. They rolled over three hundred large round bales of hay to the edge of the gulley on both sides. They had found a couple hundred gallons of diesel fuel at a farm.

Lester and Elmo asked to lead the bait boys and on the morning of the third day they were ready. The men rode in close and the zombies caught their scent, all the zombies.

Elmo thought there might be too many of them to fit in the canyon and sent one rider off to warn the ambushers. They rode back at a slow canter as the creatures ran and stumbled after them.

At the dead end of the old mine they had rigged ropes and pulleys that dropped down to the bottom of the sheer cliff. They had fastened little platforms for the men to stand on.

They rode up to the entrance and dismounted. Slapping the horse's rumps so they would run off to safety, the men ran into the decline all the way to the wall.

With three or four men on each platform they were pulled straight up to the top. It took almost an hour for all the zees to fill the man made canyon. Twenty men rode up to the entrance shooting strays and blocking the exit.

Some of them tried to climb the walls but were picked off by sharpshooters. On top, they dieseled the bales, lit them on fire and rolled them down on the heads of the crowded monsters.

They could smell that bar-b-que clear down to Texas!

They rode back towards Wichita shooting all the crippled zees that were still crawling along. There were only twenty three people left alive in all of town.

They celebrated it as a major victory and Pat got lucky again.

# CHAPTER TWENTY SIX

S am and Wolfy went over to the courthouse and walked in the Mayor's office. "Afternoon Helen," Wolfy said, "we need to talk."

He told her all about the events of the day and what news he had learned. "Your news Sheriff, appears to be all unsubstantiated hearsay." She looked right at him.

"Well, I have no reason to disbelieve either source." He stated, "Helen, Mrs. Mayor, I think we should have a whole town meeting right away. Maybe at the Presby."

Helen liked that idea, she loved being political. "7:00 pm sounds good to me, I'll have someone find the pastor and see about lights and such."

Sam and Wolfy left to inform as many citizens as they could find in a couple hours.

Pastor Thomas Smith was a thin, pale man of average height. He harbored no thoughts of being a great evangelist, with his robust and double queen sized wife, four daughters and one obnoxious cat he was content where he was.

He presided over a nice church with a steady turnout and tithing offering every week. He sermonized on the love of Christ and the evils of sin. He made no political statements and truly enjoyed the occasional wedding and christening. He gave no opinion on the same sex marriage issue and secretly prayed it would go away.

Libby Dechantre came in and gave him the Mayor's message. He smiled and told Libby to convey to the Mayor that he would get things ready right away. Thinking to himself how rude it was to volunteer his church without discussing it with him first.

No matter, he called his wife and daughters into the church and soon they were dusting and polishing.

Lights however, were a problem. He looked in the store room and found a dozen candles, not enough. In the basement were two oil lamps, still not enough.

He went next door to the hardware. He explained to Herb his problem and Herb demonstrated to him the big battery powered area lamps he had.

"Wow, they're bright. That would probably do the job, how long do the batteries last?" pastor Tom looked up with a smile.

"Forever, they're rechargeable." Herb smiled back.

"Can you put regular batteries in them? I'll pay for them and bring the lamps back tomorrow."

Herb frowned. "Can't, sold out of regular batteries this morning. Those lamps are thirty seven dollars and forty seven cents each and the recharger is an additional twenty eight fifty."

"You want one hundred and three dollars and forty four cents for those lamps?" Pastor Tom frowned.

"Plus tax." Herb smiled.

Pastor Tom wrote a check and smiled.

Herb frowned.

Sam and Wolfy talked to about thirty folks before people were asking them about the meeting and they figured they had the town covered.

Wolfy saw the semi at the Superduper earlier and had Sam drop him there so Sam could go get Arnie, Jake and Brad because he wanted them there to answer any questions the assemblage might have.

He knocked on the cab door, "Hello, anybody in there?" he called out. The door opened and Bob asked him if he wanted a sandwich. He did, the day was getting long and he had, had an early lunch.

There wasn't another seat in the sleeper but Sadie got up and moved to the passenger bucket.

"Wow," said the Sheriff, "this is some interior, leather?" Bob nodded and told him about the encounter with Miss Millie and how he moved the truck.

"That's it, that's all she said?" Wolfy asked Sadie with a look of disbelief on his face.

"Yep, turned around as nice as you please and went back in her house." Sadie was matter of fact.

"Well don't worry about her, she doesn't own this parking lot, I think." Wolfy's brow furrowed.

Then he told them about the meeting and told Bob he would probably have to tell his story again. Bob shrugged. Wolfy thanked him for the sandwich, left and walked back to his office.

Deputy Dawg was snoring with his head back and mouth open. Wolfy slammed the door. Dawg suddenly looked more alert.

"You have the prisoner booked and filed?" Dawg nodded yes, "Let me have the sheet." Wolfy held out his hand.

"You wrote his name down as Donald F N Duck?"

"That's what he told me." Pleaded Dawg.

Wolfy was pissed. He went back to the cell and there the guy was hanging by his neck from his shoestrings turning in a slow circle.

"Dawg! You're fired! Put your badge on the desk and get out! Jesus jumping jackrabbits!"

Wolfy was muttering to himself about pouring rain when he heard the door slam. He wrote down a description of the suicide scene complete with measurements and cut the body down. He left him on the floor.

No wallet, no ID, Donald F N Duck, stupid smartass. Wolfy sighed, he was stuck 'til Sam got back. He went out to his very empty office. He thought it was amazing how much room that big dummy took up.

This was the third time he had fired him this year but he wasn't coming back this time, no matter what. He royally screwed the pooch and now he had to feed the puppies.

Well, he had the fingerprints and he would have a name whenever the power came back on.

Arnie declined the ride and told Sam the meeting could be held without him. Just tell Wolfy that he was concerned that the kids were maybe coming down with something.

Sam looked over at the kids playing and laughing around Clay's swing set. "Watch 'em close," said Sam, "what their coming up with is bad enough." With that said he drove on.

Arnie walked over to the swing set. Terry and Barry were hanging upside down from the cross bar having a tickle fight with Jimmy and Clay. Sally was sitting on that thing that pivoted when you swang on it, sorta like a teeter totter.

"You kids seem to be having fun." Arnie said to her.

"Oh yes, Mr. Swende," she smiled at him, "it's important to have fun. We all think so."

"All of you?" Arnie was puzzled and waved his arm towards the boys who immediately stopped playing and looked at him.

"No, ALL of us, we've lost so very many and only had one new friend turn old enough to know now." She spoke quietly and evenly.

"I see," Arnie needed time to think, "how about all us men carry in some firewood and Sally can go help Mattie and Becca?"

He could think better, he thought, when he was doing no think work.

# CHAPTER TWENTY SEVEN

Sam, Brad and Jake were three abreast in the cab of the old GMC and on their way in when they saw the Amish buggy.

It was Levi and Malachi Byler. The brothers had adjoining farms, a saw mill, a carpentry business and thirteen sons between them. The buggy stopped and Sam pulled up.

"We heard you English lost your power." Malachi said.

"That's true enough," said Jake, "how are you and yours making out?"

"Just another day for us you know." Levi was grinning. "We're heading into town the kids say there's a big meeting going on."

"Your kids are right," Jake asserted, "at the Presbyterian Church. We'll see you there."

Sam drove on. "I wonder how their kids found out?" Jake mused. Sam said nothing.

Brad was blitzed, before Sam showed up Jake gave him a whole ounce for saving the day earlier and Brad rolled a big ass spliff. They had just finished it when Sam pulled in the driveway.

They steered around a stalled log truck and Sam turned down Sleeping Woman lane and drove to the end.

Sarey Spank lived in an old camping trailer with her blind dog and a white goat. She came out wiping her hands.

Sarey was a sort of lady hermit, didn't bother anyone except if she thought they were looking for big foot. She would try and discourage them as she told everyone that big foot had told her they didn't like being disturbed.

Sometimes, Sarey would be seen wearing her tinfoil hat to keep the alien mind probes out of her brain. Everyone had long since learned not to talk about witches or religion around her.

Sam felt it was his duty as a sworn deputy to tell her about the meeting nevertheless. Sarey's long, straight blond hair had long since turned white but she still wore fake flowers in it. Today it was a faded cloth poinsettia.

"Bad vibes today," she pointed forked fingers at the sky, "even the goat is skitterish."

Sam asked her if she wanted to attend the meeting but she begged off. She said she thought she was getting a visitor later on and looked at the forest behind her place.

"You sure it isn't us?" Jake asked her.

"No, this is the day THEY stop by." She said and walked back to her trailer.

"They?" asked Brad.

"Yeah, big eight foot tall furry things," said Jake, "You ought to ask her out. She probably hasn't had human sex in quite a while."

They all were laughing. Soon they were back in town helping Wolfy to load the dead jail bird in the truck to take to the coroner.

"You fired Dawg?" Sam asked.

"He was taking a nap on duty when that yahoo hung himself, what would you do?" Wolfy said curtly.

"But aren't we shorthanded now?" Sam wanted to know.

"We were shorthanded with him, besides Brad and Jake are going to volunteer to be temporary deputies, right?" the Sheriff's department was getting bigger.

At the church the pastor and mayor were greeting folks as they came in. they both could spread some thick honey. The pastor was thinking how he could justify a quick collection out of this, then thought it might be a little too much.

The townspeople were gathering quickly, Miss Millie came in wearing a lime green pants suit, orange shoes and a type of hat that Carmen Miranda might have favored.

The Amish men parked the buggy on the street in front of the church and the horse immediately made dirt. A big man wearing a cowboy hat and leather vest walked in accompanied by a pretty young lady. Finally Wolfy showed up with the other men in tow and the meeting was ready to start.

Wolfy opened the ball. First he thanked everyone for being there on such short notice and hoped they were all okay. He addressed the power outage, the automobile problem and then told them it looked like a long time before those problems were solved.

He introduced Bob and left him tell his own story. Miss Millie never said a word, yet. When Brad got up and said the words "planet wide" there were some gasps and mutterings.

Brad looked over at Bob and saw Sadie for the first time. I'm sure you've heard of love at first sight, maybe even experienced it for yourself. This was a classic case. Albeit a one sided classic case, there it was.

Brad stumbled and almost fell coming down from the podium, he couldn't take his eyes off Sadie.

That's when Pastor Tom's four daughters walked up in step, turned to the audience and said, "We are here to tell you the truth, all around you is death. There is no government. You must help yourselves as we will help you until the others arrive."

At that thirty four more children walked in and up to the raised platform filling the choir space and they all spoke in unison, "We see as one, we speak as one, we are one."

Every eye watched in silence as they turned and filed out in step, evenly spaced apart right past Levi and Malachi who were standing by the door but would not enter the church.

More silence.

Madam Mayor spoke first, "Does anyone know what is going on here?"

Herb the hardware man asked, "What do they mean, no government, no help?"

Jake wanted to know who the others were that were going to arrive. Pastor Tom went to find his daughters and get some answers.

Wolfy looked at Sam who had his head bowed and his hands covering his face. Brad looked at Sadie who looked away.

Wolfy took to the rostrum, "Now everybody has questions, who has any answers?"

Wade K said, "It was like that old movie about the blond haired kids, only those were our children."

Judge Reinholt, a retired federal district court appointee spoke up, "Parents should question their children individually. If this was some kind of prank or a hoax we need to know right away." The Mayor agreed and ended the meeting.

That night they learned the awful truth, one child at a time. The coronal mass ejection, the plague of mutated flu, the demise of the government, they were on their own.

The town council met the next morning. "But not one of them could or would say anything about these so called others except that they were coming." Mayor Helen said.

Wade spoke up, "They did insinuate that we are isolated from the worst of the calamity, therefore we should take steps to protect and defend our town as well as ourselves."

Brandi Nutters, who owned The Olde Curiosity Shoppe asked, "How do we do that? Block off the roads, build barricades, post armed guards?"

"Exactly," said Judge Reinholt, "now who do we have with military experience?"

"There's my Joe," said Helen, "Wolfy was an MP, the men at the VFW, they will know others."

"Okay then," said Wade, "Judge, would you inform Wolfy? Helen, I know you know where Joe is?"

Oddly, Millie Beachum hadn't said a word. Wade ended the meeting.

Helen found Joe behind the bar at the VFW, sitting on the stool that had supported him for many years. She told him all that had transpired and asked him what he thought.

He wondered why she had asked him. Other than cleaning and doing maintenance at the laundry mat, he spent the majority of his time right where he was, doing nothing. Then he realized she must really be frightened.

He told her to relax, he'd get the rest of the club members together and they would work as they had been trained to keep everybody safe.

She hugged him and laid her head on his shoulder. She didn't speak.

# CHAPTER TWENTY EIGHT

George was looking at a photograph of his father. The unsmiling face stared back at him like it had once stared at the camera.

The man was in prison on a vehicular manslaughter charge. Like so many people of his tribe he was a drinker, a drinker who drove.

George barely remembered him. He fingered the amulet that now hung around his neck, it caused him some apprehension. After all, he was still pretty young.

He walked out of the home into the bright, hot sunlight, shielding his eyes from the glare. His sister was tending the fire and cooking something in a large pot.

They heard an awful noise and looking up saw a huge airliner pass right over their heads and then crash on the mesa above them.

The whole family climbed up the steep trail to the top. There was still burning wreckage when they arrived, debris scattered in a long path.

They walked slowly forward. Sarah, George's sister who was fourteen was already crying. Their mother cautioned them not to touch anything as the government would be there soon to investigate.

Grandfather said it had taken them an hour to climb up and that they should have already been here. There were vultures overhead turning in large, slow circles.

The plane had broken into several sections, on the tail was the letters KAL. They saw bodies ripped apart and burnt. Suitcases, clothing, seats all jumbled up and spread out.

They looked for two hours, no one was alive. They touched nothing. No one came either. They heard no search craft or desert vehicles.

George was looking at a toy stuffed dog when the man in white appeared in his head and told him why the plane had crashed.

He stood rock still for many minutes, then finally turned to his grandfather and said, "The sun caused this it has affected the whole world."

Grandfather raised his arms to the sky and beseeched the spirits to care for the many souls who were lost on the mesa.

They left to return home before dark. George carried the toy dog with him. That evening Grandfather told him that by obeying the vision of Maasau'u the God, who told him to reject the white man's ways and live apart that they were safe.

He told George that he must also heed the visions he receives. George told him his visions were of violence, death and chaos but also of a great joy in the heavens.

The old man told of prophecies made long ago, the omens of the past few years and said that this must be the time of the Gods.

# CHAPTER TWENTY NINE

T he Free Rangers of Kansas became their official name after Wichita. The entourage was growing even more after Wellington and Arkansas City.

One hundred and fifty strong men and women, black, white, red and Asian. They, in many respects resembled a medieval army with all the camp followers and animals that tagged along.

Sheila had been keeping a log, now three notebooks long. They had lost twenty four deputies by then but had killed thousands and saved hundreds of lives.

The children with them remained strangely quiet, speaking only when spoken to or asked a question. They would all stand still at times and stare off in the distance. The doctor with them said it was probably situational shock.

They stopped at the state line this is where Pat and Sheila's authority ended. After a discussion with the war council the decision was made to continue on to Oklahoma City and persevere.

They swept through Blackwell like a roiling storm of thunder and death. They had learned to duct tape magazines and telephone books to their arms and legs after seeing one feller doing it. He told them he had seen it in some lame zombie movie. Go figure.

In Ponca City Sheila's horse stepped in a hole. Thrown off and stunned the zees moved in for the kill. Once again, Elmo McMurdy came to the rescue!

Leaping his stud right into the bodies of the attackers he shot his guns empty. Dropping them he pulled two more from his waistband and emptied them as well. His stallion leapt and kicked spinning and hopping in a mad rush of fury. Others rushed in to help, Sheila was saved.

In Stillwater they discovered the aftermath of the bird flu. Everyone was dead, the zombies were still human enough to succumb to it as well. It was a sobering sight.

Oklahoma City was silent the only things moving were the flags and the banners of used car lots. Business was slow.

They dared not enter the towns for fear that they might catch whatever it was that killed so many and they decided to turn west.

They picked up what supplies they could forage but it appeared that all were dead along I-40. They turned back north at highway 81 and found more zees in Enid and an embattled family that were almost out of hope.

The zombies were beginning to die off from hunger and exposure. They kept on searching and found pockets of healthy humans they were able to save.

In two more weeks it was over. Freezing temperatures and snow moved in to destroy the exposed infected. They rode back to Hays.

Pat and Sheila were married by reverend Craig Bruce, the only preacher left. Those still left with them witnessed the rites. Elmo was the best man.

They found a house that had been abandoned and struggled to keep warm and fed all while keeping a constant vigil just in case.

They stopped at the CDC compound but found nothing. All the lab animals were dead, the carcasses burnt. They did find three rooms that contained beds with tie down straps and autopsy tables, undoubtedly used on humans. Sheila had to run outside and stood there bent over and shuddering. They set the place on fire.

One morning not long after, Sheila answered the door and there was Bobbie Sue Mack, Zack McIntire, and Larry Reedy Bill's little boy.

She let them in and they sat by the wood stove. The children spoke in unison to her about the state of the world. They answered all her questions as best they could. They told her to be patient, the dangers had passed and the Others were coming and soon would be there.

# CHAPTER THIRTY

R oad trip! Those joyous words have a whole new meaning now thought Gary as he watched Addie secure a car seat for Sasha.

Even though he had been obdurate about leaving on the wishes of a three year old, after observing Sasha go off in some thought where she sat very still and stared ahead then told them about things she couldn't possibly have known Gary acquiesced.

The tank was full and they had a spare five gallons, plenty of goodies and a 9mm handgun which Addie kept in her waistband. They were off.

Taking route 111 they were lucky with relatively clear lanes but they had to navigate around and through Indio where they picked up I-10. Slowly they picked their way along. There were several wrecked semis at one point and they crossed the medial to pass.

Stopping at a rest area they took an extended break. Sasha ran and played while Gary and Addie talked getting to know each other better.

Addie told him about her parents and three brothers, growing up in Compton, the army nursing school and her last boyfriend.

He told her about his mother, lover, and pranks that students had pulled on him down through the years.

Another vehicle pulled in and parked beside the Falcon. Gary hurried to get Sasha and Addie pulled out the gun and switched the safety off.

A man and a boy got out. A forty something year old Hispanic fellow, wearing a straw hat and a young Asian boy of about seven. Standing nervously, they both waved and said hello.

Addie wasn't taking any chances, raising the slide action weapon she said, "Hands in the air, walk forward, stop, turn around." She saw no weapons, approached and quickly frisked them, they were clean.

She backed up five paces and lowered the gun. "Okay, turn back around now. You can lower your arms."

Gary, now holding Sasha peered from around the building. Sasha saw the two and squirmed to get free yelling, "Ollie! Ollie!"

Oliver Ying smiled and said, "Sasha."

The Hispanic gentleman's name was Umberto Gomez, a migrant farm hand and fruit picker. He had been driving his 1964 Impala when he spied Oliver walking along the road.

Oliver had told him he was going to San Luis Obispo, Umberto had nowhere else to go so . . . He had lost his wife, children, family, now he had Ollie.

Gary questioned him closely about what Ollie had said and done while they had been together and learned the two children's behavior was the same.

"It appears we are witnessing a new phenomenon in human communication." Gary said with awe. "A telepathic collective mind set."

"But why only children? Professor," Addie asked.

"Why indeed, young lady?" the professor thought for a moment, "perhaps it has something to do with sexuality or hormones, honestly I don't know."

"El trebajo del Diablo, the work of the devil senor," said Umberto making the sign of the cross.

"Would they have private thoughts, free will?" Addie wondered.

"I don't know about that but they are playing hide and go seek right now. Just think, a step in evolution, a totally new way to do business if you pardon my colloquialism. Everyone would have no choice but to be honest. No need for laws, trials, guarantees or politicians. There could be no deception, a new age of innocence." Gary was looking off and holding his chin.

"That sounds like an ideal world to live in." Addie opined.

"Yes, we must protect these children at all costs. They are the future and a very bright future it will be." Gary slapped his knees,

"Now we should be moving along, I can't wait to see what's in San Luis O."

They drove on to route 62, on to 247 into Barstow. They stopped to scrounge gas. Finally they were on route 58 which went through Bakersfield but ended up in San Luis Obispo.

They saw no people, live people that is. The dead were everywhere, the scavengers were feasting. Packs of dogs, whom had until just recently had been someone's beloved pet stalked them as they drove slowly along. The smells were horrid.

Finally at dusk they stopped for the night and built a fire. Umberto went to scavenge and Addie was cooking dinner. A half a moon rose in the night sky and it became cool.

The next day they drove through what had been a large wildfire. Both sides of the road and in places the blacktop itself had burnt. There were several burned out vehicles along the way and some blackened corpses also.

They drove for nearly an hour through the ash, at one point the road was completely blocked by wreckage and they had to backtrack and use country lanes to bypass it.

The children didn't mind riding in separate cars and Gary and Addie carried on light conversation. Sometimes Sasha would start to giggle for no reason. At long last they saw a sign, San Luis Obispo 12 miles.

When they entered the town there was a big sign saying, "Welcome to San Luis Obispo, the happiest place in the world." A beautiful place on a beautiful day except for the dead, it was perfect.

They found a very nice motel and took rooms on the ground floor. Addie and the kids in one and the men chose one each.

Addie set up the cook stove and made a wonderful concoction using spam, vegies and potatoes. To Gary's chagrin there were wine shops everywhere. Unlike most towns there was no evidence of looting.

Umberto returned from his scouting excursion with a hunting rifle and another handgun. "We have been lucky so far senor," he said to Gary, "but it is not wise to push the luck, no?" Gary, who was sampling a delicious local Chablis agreed. They had a very pleasant evening.

The next morning, after a breakfast of fruit the children said they must go to the beach. Addie found a nice bikini in a boutique with a big floppy sun hat. She wrapped a length of silk around her hips and was dazzling.

She checked the price tags on the items and laughed. They were more than she had earned in a month.

But the kids didn't want to go to the sand, they pointed out a spot on top of the cliffs where a sheer drop to wave splashed rocks tested everyone's nerve.

The children sat down and merely waited, looking out towards the ocean. Gary was watching the water also, feeling the sea breeze on his face when all of a sudden something began to rise up out of the surf.

It was huge, a curved arc, a giant swollen boomerang! At least three hundred yards across and fifty thick, the wings tapered and curled it rose silently out of the Pacific.

"The Others." said Sasha and Ollie. It was jet black yet seemed luminous, solid yet flexible like silly putty. It rose above them, flew over and gently landed on the flat ground behind them.

Addie felt trapped, backs to the cliff and the craft between them and the car. (They had all rode with Umberto). The children were still sitting as calm as could be.

Gary's mouth hung open, for once in his life he was utterly speechless. He had seen that shape before, carved in stone above a dancing Mayan man on the main pyramid in Copan.

And thus, the first contact with interstellar travelers was made in the idyllic, happiest place in the world.

# CHAPTER THIRTY ONE

Becca, Arnie, and Mattie listened as the children spoke. They didn't know it then but it was an exact recital at the same time that was being said at the town meeting.

"Clay, honey," Mattie said to her son, "how can you know all this? Who are these others?"

Clay pointed to his head, "We just know, in here. I can see, hear, feel, taste, and smell everything everyone else does if I want to."

"Everyone?" asked Arnie.

Sally spoke up, "Every kid like us, we can only know feelings from you grownups. Like we know you're afraid right now."

Becca gasped, "This is unnatural."

Jimmy looked at her, "No ma'am, it is very natural. The Others told us we could always do it but had a block in our brains, it's gone now."

Mattie said, "You still haven't answered my question. Who or what are these others?"

The next morning Wolfy and his deputies were at the VFW. Joe Stroup was at his usual station behind the bar and there were fourteen other men there as well. They had a big, framed map of the township hanging on the wall.

"If we block all three bridges and set up a barricade where Pigeon Hill road meets the highway, that leaves only German Hill still open." Ken Wineheart pointed out.

Ken had been a Captain in Viet Nam commanding a rifle company. Now retired, like many residents of Tionesta. He had been living there for four years now having moved from Ohio.

"German Hill is a problem," Wolfy said, "so is the river. Jack, can we put a man up in your lighthouse?"

Jack Sheetz owned two self storage businesses, ran a handyman slash landscape outfit and owned the island in the middle of the river. He had won a half million in the state lottery and for some unknown reason had built a full sized lighthouse on the island. He charged two bucks a head to people who wanted to climb the hundred or so steps to see the view. He had been a navy man.

"Absolutely," he responded with enthusiasm, "that is a perfect lookout place. Only they got to clean it up if there's a mess. People leave the strangest stuff up there, cans, condoms . . . ."

"Thanks Jack!" Ken interrupted, he knew where that was going. "Okay, guns. I trust everyone in this room has a shotgun at least or a twenty two. Bring it, keep it handy. If you need ammo there's some at the hardware." This was met with a groan as Herb kept his prices pretty high on that stuff, well, all stuff.

The Judge spoke up, "I'll personally tell him to keep a record and that he will be paid from the towns emergency fund."

"You'll need to think about what to do if any refugees show up. That flu those kids told us about can be a worse enemy than the Japs." This from Cyrus Bookwalter, at Ninety one he was the oldest veteran.

A former marine officer, he served for the entire length of World War Two. He survived four invasions of Japanese held islands including Iwo Jima. He received two purple hearts, one bronze star and one silver star. They listened when he talked.

"We'd have to quarantine them somehow, can we have some suggestions?" Ken asked and the men started discussing all kinds of things from what to use to block off the roads to setting booby traps using propane tanks to shoot at. Some of the stuff got resolved.

Brad and Jake had to go home. Brad, to get his small arsenal. Jake, to get Mary and feed his rabbits.

Wolfy, Ken and the other vets who could went to get more help, guns, bullets and whatever. The post had an antique Willys Jeep gotten from surplus, circa Korean War era. It ran, they usually only drove it in parades.

There was the obligatory small field piece in front of the club but the barrel had been filled in with lead. Cyrus had a couple hand grenades but was afraid to move them, they were pretty old. Like him.

Ken was driving Wolfy in the Jeep now so Sam took Brad and Jake back up German Hill. They stopped at Arnies place and told him all the new developments. Arnie was staying put. He had food, water, heat, a couple rifles and he could watch German Hill road for travelers.

Becca told Sam she was staying put too, Mattie would need help with all the kids and chores. Goofy barked once and wagged his tail.

Brad got Arnie off to one side and told him about all the food stashed under the camp, just in case.

Mary was more than willing to go so Brad ended up riding in the truck bed.

Wolfy and Ken stopped by the big Western Star to get Bob and Sadie. Ken was admiring the art work on the trailer when he asked off hand what Bob was hauling in there.

"Don't rightly know," said Bob, "I've been under a government contract for the past year. I never see the load, the bills always say 'property US government'. I back it up to the dock, stay in the cab, pull it ahead a little to let the warehouseman lock and seal the doors. Then it's a reversal of that process at the destination."

Wolfy said that since this was an emergency situation he was using his authority to open the doors and see if what was inside could be useful. Bob broke the seal and opened up.

"What the heck are those things?" asked Ken. Stacked to the roof were what appeared to be black plastic tubs.

Wolfy read the writing on the front of one, "One, (1), emergency human remains container, must be properly sealed, FEMA."

Coffins. Bob and Sadie stood with their mouths open. Wolfy said, "Let's unload some, the coroner needs a few right now."

Stacked like plastic cups and squeezed together they had a hard time getting the first stack off and then had to find the lids. They were easier to handle.

Ken left in the Jeep and then returned pulling a trailer and they loaded ten coffin kits up for the coroner. There was room for two bodies stacked in each one.

The lids had instructions on how to seal them. Place remains in container. Use rubber mallet to engage seal lock. Simple. Morbid. The coroner was glad to get them but had to get a mallet from the hardware. Herb was a busy guy.

The bird flu, still raging like a runaway fire was encroaching on Tionesta. Having wiped out Pittsburgh and Erie it was on its way to meet up with the wave coming from the east coast.

Using the Jeep and a tow chain along with lots of man power they succeeded in blocking the bridges and highway with stalled cars. A stalled car was also quite useful as a guard post. Some folks wouldn't give up their cars but many others had no problem. The men were careful not to damage the vehicles regardless.

Bill McCready was up in the lighthouse when he spotted the first body in the river floating along. His teenage son Junior was with him and got sent to notify the Sheriff. By the time he went down the stairs, paddled across the river channel and found the lawman the body had long since passed from sight.

It was old Cyrus who thought about using the kids as telepathic communicators. He said the kids could call themselves the Navajos.

They asked for volunteers and each kid got a blue VFW baseball cap. Some parents insisted on accompanying their son or daughter and that's how a child ended up at every post.

# CHAPTER THIRTY TWO

Dawg was pissed, even after a good night's sleep. He'd been fired before but this time was different.

So what if that lowlife dirt bag hung himself. I had to walk back there TWICE and STAND to do the paperwork. He said his name was Donald F N Duck, what else was I supposed to write down?

Sleeping? Not me, I was resting after all the exertion. Dawg, not being totally stupid helped himself to a couple bags of that powder Wolfy left lying there forgotten. Call it severance pay, yeah that makes it alright. I can sell the stuff myself.

At home with his mother he got the understanding and comfort he needed. His mother was a small mousey woman. How she ever gave birth to such a giant we'll never know.

In his room, Dawg hefted one of the bags of bath salts. He wondered what pleasures people found in such substances. He knew Jake smoked weed and weed was a dangerous drug but Jake seemed normal.

He opened the bag, sniffed, no odor. He tasted a little bit, bitter, no effect. He laid out a little line like he had seen done on a DARE video. Snort, nothing.

He laid out a bigger line, he felt something. Two Big Lines! MORE!!! YEAH MORE!!!!!

His mother heard him come in the kitchen. She was cooking his favorite chicken soup. She turned with a smile to say something but found her face held down in the near boiling broth and noodles. She tried to scream, it was the last thing she ever did.

He came out of the house, his scalded hand unknown to his miscombobblated brain. Only one thought, WOLFY, HE WAS GONNA EAT WOLFY!

Wolfy however, was at the other side of town with Bob and Sadie. They were in the Superduper with Wade looking at the failing generator.

"Sounds like the rings in that thing are as worn out as an old cliché," said Bob, "it's a matter of time is all."

"But if it dies then all the frozen foods will thaw out and spoil." Wade lamented, "Nobody else has a generator this big."

Wolfy said, "I don't know."

"I know," Bob spoke up, "my trailer has a reefer unit that runs great. We unload the coffins, then if or when this thing gives up the ghost, we load the food in there and keep it frozen. I think the tank on the unit is full."

"Problem solved." Wolfy said clapping his hands.

They were shoving the stacks of plastic body containers off the truck on to the ground. It certainly didn't hurt them. It made a messy pile but it could be straightened out later.

They were over half way when they heard a scream and shouting from the middle of town. Michelle McVee was in the path of the huge, naked man lumbering down the main street, he backhanded her out of the way breaking her neck.

Herb came out of the front of the hardware store and saw Dawg in his birthday suit kill Michelle then ran back in locking the door.

Wolfy ran up to the street and Dawg spotted him. It was the first time in years Dawg had ran. Coming at Wolfy like a runaway train highballing for hell, Dawg let out a scream.

With the instincts learned in Desert Storm the Sheriff pulled his service piece and emptied it into the crazed goliath. It only slowed him down, there was a shot from behind Wolfy and Dawg's head blew apart.

Sadie had shot him with Bob's shotgun loaded with double ought buck. She stood there shaking as Bob came up from behind and gently took the gun from her hands.

Sam, Brad and Jake showed up a couple minutes later. Everybody was a little shocked. Wolfy thanked Sadie for probably saving his life but she didn't act like she heard him. Brad started over to her but she went into Bob's arms instead.

The very busy coroner came and pronounced Dawg and it took four men to get him in one of the FEMA coffins. They had to lay it on its side and roll him in then tip it upright.

"What's that on his dick?" Jake asked. It was a small tattoo that said "suck me".

"Gross!" said a girl's voice. It was Susie Smith the pastor's daughter. She told Wolfy she was to stay with him now as his communicator. The coroner was looking at Michelle and signaling for another coffin.

Sam said he'd go tell Dawg's mother. He was back in fifteen minutes to get the coroner and another coffin. "She was on the kitchen floor," he told Wolfy, "got noodles hanging out her nose. I found this in his bedroom." He produced the one and a half bags of dope.

That was when Susie tugged on Wolfy's sleeve and said someone was coming. She pointed towards the barricade at the end of town.

It was Reatha Seeker and two small children. She lived in Endeavor which was five miles away not far from Sally Pinker's house.

Ralph Lipton made them stop fifty feet back from the blockage. "Quit pointing that gun at me Ralphie, you know better." Reatha called out, "You wanta hurt one of these kids?"

"They belonged to Bill and Mercy Peete 'til he went and shot her and then blew his brains out last night." She waved her hands over the kid's heads and said, "Orphans."

The children stood there in silence looking at Jarrod Potts and young Susie who had just got there. Jarrod was the eight year old telepath at that post.

The Sheriff spoke up, "How'er things in Endeavor Reatha?"

"Fair, considering." Reatha came back, "What's all this?" she said indicating the barricade.

"There's a bad, killer flu going 'round, we're trying to keep it out."

"I ain't heard nothing 'bout that. These kids been yammering away about all kinds of foolishness, said they had to come here."

"There's a problem Reatha." Wolfy went on to tell her about how they didn't know who she had been in contact with or who those folks had been in contact with and they couldn't let her or the kids in for seventy two hours.

Reatha asked him if she had to stand there for three days with nervous young men pointing guns at her when Susie tugged on his sleeve again and said, "Its' okay Mr. Culpepper, we know they're alright." Jarrod nodded.

Wolfy looked at the kids and then called out, "Reatha, you been around any sick folk lately?"

"Physically no, mentally yes."

"Come on then, I know you wouldn't lie," and he waved her through.

The next morning they set tents up outside the lines.

# CHAPTER THIRTY THREE

Stunned, frightened, calm with foreknowledge, these were the mixed emotions of the little band of travelers. The craft did nothing, it sat there.

Sasha and Ollie stood up and with a come on motion made with their hands they began to walk towards it. The adults stepped forward with trepidation.

Umberto was reciting "Hail Mary" in Spanish but had a calm look on his face. Addie kept shooting Gary looks like, 'are you allowing this?', "you sure this is safe?'.

When they got within twenty yards of it a change in the color and density of a wide oval area began. Soon an opening appeared, seeming like an ancient cave entrance. Three human shaped beings stepped into the sunlight.

Addie thought to herself that they seemed very human. She heard words that did not use sound. "Yes Addie, you are correct. We do look very human because we are what you call 'human'."

The voice she heard was neither male nor female it was calm and soothing, familiar yet foreign. They, one male and two females came forward and stopped.

Ollie and Sasha were smiling and holding out their arms. Umberto stepped in front of the children protectively. Unspoken words were heard by all, "Fear not Umberto, we will not harm the children or yourself."

Ollie touched his arm and said, "It's okay, they love each one of us."

The male looked at Gary and again in that soundless voice said, "You are correct Professor, you have seen depictions of our craft before as well as the many different models we have created. Come and enter within, all will be explained to you."

Gary muttered, "In for a penny . . ." They entered in to what proved to be a lovely garden. Fruit trees, some recognizable, some not. Beautiful flowers again some they knew, some unknown.

Gary noticed that above them was a simulated blue sky with clouds that radiated light. He was impressed. There were stone and wooden benches and all were bade to sit.

Small grey creatures, so often depicted as aliens in modern lore entered the area carrying trays of drinks and what turned out to be tollhouse cookies.

When everyone was settled and the children were happily munching away Gary remarked that his drink tasted like a pink champagne he had once tried that he thought quite delicious.

Addie said hers tasted like chilled cranberry juice, Umberto smacked his lips and said, Mango, my favorite."

The disembodied voice said that the containers could sense your flavor desires and change the molecules of base water. Sasha giggled with a chocolate milk mustache. The beings smiled at them and the voice in their heads began.

"Your present race has been almost totally destroyed. This has happened several times in the long saga of humanity. We first arose from evolution and gene mutation over twelve hundred million years ago.

The first and greatest civilization which is who we are had taken medicine and technology to the point that our life spans were unending. Physical work became obsolete. Exercise through competition and sex a joy. Our science made interstellar travel a fact and we set off to explore the galaxy.

In our three hundred thousandth year an enormous comet entered the solar system. It passed close enough to the gas giant you call Jupiter that gravity caused it to fracture and split in half. The twin comets raced side by side to the sun. As they reached perihelion the sun's gravitational force shattered them. There were thousands of fragments.

Our compatriots tried in vain to deflect or destroy them but failed. We witnessed the destruction with horror through the eyes of our fellow men and women until the images and screaming in our minds stopped. Those of us scattered in space were too far away to affect a rescue in time.

The huge pieces struck the Earth with such force that the planet's crust was broken and the Earth was turned on its axis. The island continent where most of the civilization was centered was moved from its tropical climate much like your present Hawaii to the southpole where it still lies.

The single great land mass was cracked and set adrift on floating plates that caused the separate continents you have today. Mountain ranges pushed up, volcanoes erupted, deserts were created. Only the creatures of the oceans survived.

Some of us returned, our population reduced to sixty million throughout the galaxy. We decided to recolonize, only something was wrong. The children born on Earth could not communicate with us, none of them. They could only utilize a small percentage of their brains.

We ran tests, we searched for answers. Their offspring fared no better. We tried cloning but those created on the planet suffered the same defect. We search for the answer to this awful puzzle to this day.

How incredibly ironic that here on our home world, is now the one place in all of known creation where this phenomenon takes place.

We allowed those men on the planet to live and flourish but the inability to fully communicate undid them time and time again. It remains an enigma, this . . . something we are missing but now to sense the fresh minds of all these children means our efforts must be redoubled. The solution is at hand.

It is embarrassing actually for fourteen trillion minds working in concert not to find the answer. We are human however and we know mistakes are inevitable.

We would allow mankind to rule themselves. We would not interfere with their decisions but deceit, envy, hate, greed and fear traits that we cannot fathom. That only exist in closed and unenlightened minds would destroy many and sometimes all the lives they infest.

Insanity is known to us as a curable disease, to the inhabitants of Earth it seems it is desirable. If you would like an example we would show you nuclear weapons, true insanity.

Used in your distant past in what you call India and Gobi. In your common era in what you call New Mexico, Nevada, Japan, Russia, North Korea and Bimini.

At times we would make limited contact. We would be hailed as Gods but our teachings reviled and discarded or worse forgotten. Time and time again civilization rose to lofty heights only to be thwarted over and over.

We observed, apparently the only thing we could do short of subjugation which we will never do. Yet we held out hope, hope that more than just a scattered few would understand that your lives and your environment were all that truly mattered."

Sasha and Ollie were not only hearing these words in their minds but they saw the images, felt the emotions, smelt the truth. From them the children around the globe experienced this also. With their minds open now they could understand and fully grasp these ideals.

"Yes, for some unknown reason a man created on Earth since the first extinction has had this blockage in the brain. We have been unable to discover why.

The subsequent and present editions of man kinds attempt to achieve greatness only use one tenth of your brain capacity, we, with our minds united use the entire volume of our craniums as was always intended. We have our private lives and our universal lives."

Addie wished to ask a question, "But where is the proof, the ruins, the fossils, the garbage heaps?"

"All around you, you see them everyday. The pyramids of Egypt date back one million years, far longer than your archeologists thought. The Sphinx is double that age. The Ica stones of Peru date back seventy million years when men walked with dinosaurs.

In your Texas are fossilized footprints of man and tyrannosaurus rex side by side. Who was hunting who is open to speculation. Men discover strange things yet write them off as anomalies. Ruins beneath the seas, gold chains incased in coal, objects on the moon, metal objects found in geodes. Truly you have barely scratched the surface of all that lies hidden on and around the Earth.

What you call Hudson Bay is a crater from the time of the twin comets. The powers that be or were rather, feared the truth and kept it suppressed. We came to aid our offspring and they called us Gods then despised us for what we taught. This happened over and over again."

Gary was listening but also observing the beings. The man was about six feet tall, he had an athletic build, white hair, blue eyes with an Asian caste and a cropped white beard.

Dressed in what appeared to be white pajama like cotton pants and shirt he wore a large blue teardrop shaped diamond on a gold chain around his neck.

The females were also dressed in this fashion with the same jewelry. All three looked to be about thirty years of age.

Gary had a question, "Sir, are there only the three of you?"

The man looked at him and the voice returned to their heads, "No, there are four hundred of us on this ship, we have four more ships here on the planet and fourteen trillion unique beings spread across the galaxy."

"Another question please," Gary asked, "you stated earlier that you can sustain your bodies indefinitely, are you immortal?"

"No, we die as easily as you from accident."

"But what if you are attacked by some other beings?" Gary asked again.

"There is no one to attack us, in our journeys across and deep into our galaxy we have found no one. There is life in abundance but no creatures with cognizant minds. Accidents occur however no matter how safe a person conducts themselves. We have decided to reveal ourselves completely to this human epoch because of the children who have finally overcome the blockage of their minds and can join us in our unity.

We wish to educate them, study them and celebrate their enlightenment, this is a joyous occasion for us."

At that Sasha and Ollie arose and walked to him, he put his hands on their shoulders and spoke aloud for the first time, "We will start with these two."

# CHAPTER THIRTY FOUR

On the day the power went out George Fryburg was driving the Blue Goose. A prison transport bus with sixteen shackled inmates and another guard, Richard Pugh. They were on their way to the State Correctional Facility at Marionville.

They were close to their destination when the bus stalled and George steered it to the berm. "Sit tight ladies, we'll get this figured out," Officer Pugh smirked to the chained men.

After an hour of failed starts and no radio contact with anyone and no traffic for that matter, the two guards had a problem. The inmates wanted to relieve themselves.

Pugh was armed with a shotgun, sidearm, taser, mace and nightstick. Fryburg had a sidearm. They had just entered the national forest and there were no buildings in sight.

"One at a time, or all at once," Officer Fryburg asked the duty guard.

"Help can come at any minute. I say keep them all chained together and let them have a pissing contest." Sergeant Pugh decided.

The guards were responsible for the bus and didn't want to be scrubbing inmate urine off the seats and floor. Shackled at the ankles with a common chain connecting them and with individual handcuffs the odds were good for no trouble.

Rocky Grossman was seeing the last of the outside world. In Pennsylvania a life sentence meant that they kept your body an extra day to make sure you served all your time.

He was second in line as they all stood there and peed. Beside him was Lonny Walter, a small ratty looking man who had raped his son and daughter for several years.

Rocky had one chance. Officer Pugh was holding the shotgun facing the rapist. Rocky directed his stream on the smaller man's leg. He started to jerk back and yell, Pugh stepped forward to stop it.

Rocky made a grab for the gun which went off into Mr. Walter. Rocky tore it out of the surprised guard's hands, worked the pump and shot Pugh before he could draw another weapon.

The prisoner at the other end of the line, a huge black man with the name of Jamal Jackson caught Fryburg as he started towards the trouble and strangled him with his handcuffs. The man beside him struck the guard in the stomach and grabbed the pistol and shot him.

Pugh had the keys and the criminals were soon free. Not knowing where they were they chose to run into the woods towards the west. After ten minutes of running they stopped.

Rocky had the shotgun but there was only one shell left. The man who held Pugh's sidearm was a thin drug dealer from Beaver Falls named Quince. The other gun was in the possession of Frankie Brown who had beat his wife to death with a ballpeen hammer.

Lucas Leekus, a small time car thief was looking at the taser he held. "Man, how dis ting work?" he said just before it fired the darts into his chest. As he lay there spasming among the leaves the others all had a laugh. "Stupid shit." One of them said.

Rocky, who had shot two tellers and a cop during a botched bank robbery said that something must have happened. He pointed out that the radio on the bus wouldn't work and that absolutely no traffic had come down the road the whole time they were there. He also told them they had to get out of the orange jumpsuits they were wearing.

"Okay Einstein, we in da woods. How we gonna do dat?" Jamal wanted to know.

"We have to find a house or something." Rocky said and they walked on through the forest.

They came upon a series of hunting camps which were unoccupied but they got a few clothes and a bow with arrows. They also found four bottles of liquor. Then they came to a farmhouse.

Two of them, (one was Quince) were wearing pilfered cammos and went and knocked on the door. When a man opened up to ask what they wanted they shot him. They rushed in finding the man's wife and teenaged daughter.

After all the rest of them had crowded into the house they made the woman cook for them as a few of them raped the daughter in the next room.

After eating, they ransacked the house the mother falling victim to rape as well. Two deer rifles and a twelve gauge shotgun added to their arsenal. They then killed the two women and left their prison clothes behind.

One of the former cons wanted to leave on his own. Jamal shot him in the back as he walked away and then cut his throat with an old breadknife.

They stayed in the woods just off the road to keep out of sight of traffic that never came. Now numbering fourteen they acknowledged Rocky as their leader. They stayed in an empty camp that night finding more alcohol.

After they left there they saw a road sign that said Tionesta, 6 miles. "What'd you think?" Frankie asked Rocky.

"Maybe, we need more stuff first. Let's do a little more sacking and pillaging, see what else we can pick up. It seems to be working good for us so far."

They split up. Two seven man teams, Rocky of course led one and Jamal the other. There are a lot of camps and semi isolated homes in the forest area and the crews stayed busy for two days.

They were pushing wheelbarrows and pulling cart full of bullets and shells, liquor and food, clothes, flashlights, all kinds of crap. Going right down the middle of the road, as they were emboldened by then.

They came together at the top of Church Hill road. They had terrorized an old geezer named Scott into drawing them a map of the area the day before. As payment they crushed his skull with a sledgehammer.

Quince was wearing some ridiculous neon pink hat with a sunflower on it, Jamal toted two twelve gauge shotguns he had sawn off with a hacksaw along with two belts full of shells.

Only one of them was still unarmed, a short stocky accountant with glasses and a bald spot. He had robbed one of his clients of eighty grand, he carried a machete.

All in all there were sixteen bodies along their back trail. They couldn't believe their luck that no cops were looking for them but then they couldn't find a running car either.

They had stayed pretty well drunk the whole time, not eating much and doing whatever they wanted to their victims. The more they did the worse they got, trying to outdo each others depravity.

Next they figured to take over an entire town. Tionesta. Rocky told them his plan.

# CHAPTER THIRTY FIVE

B ob was hurting, a dull ache in his chest. His left arm was sore and he felt sick to his stomach. He took another blood pressure pill and a couple aspirins. He was afraid this was it, the big one, I'm coming 'Lisbeth. Like that old red something comic used to say.

Sadie was concerned the drug store hadn't been open so she was in the grocery trying to find something that would help. There was no doctor in town, only a walk in clinic and it wasn't open the day the power went out. It had been a busy four days.

Sadie was in the over the counter meds isle when Brad walked up to her. "Hi," he said, "you were pretty impressive yesterday stopping that maniac."

"I killed a man. I don't want to talk about it." Sadie put it bluntly.

"Is there something about me you don't like, are you a Ravens fan?" Brad was smiling at her.

Sadie looked at him then, he was a good looking guy, he saved those two old hippies and stopped a drug ring. "No, I'm not a Rave . . ." the lights went out again.

Wade and Heather the cashier were looking at the generator when Brad and Sadie walked in the back. "I'm afraid the goose is cooked." Wade was shaking his head. There was an odor of burnt motor oil and a thin line of smoke was rising from the top of the machine. Visible in the flashlight beam that Heather held.

"We need to use the truck now." Wade said in a defeated manner.

"There's more coffins on the truck yet," Sadie said as she looked at Brad, "give a lady a hand Steelers fan?"

Ken Wineheart pulled up to the semitrailer in the army jeep. With him was Jake, Mary and little Penny Totters their communicator. Wade explained what needed to be done and Penny sent out the message.

Soon there were about ten men and women there to help transfer the frozen food. First however, the rest of the coffins had to come out.

The men pushed and grunted as they slid them off and others got them out of the way. The last stack were half size, Jake said they must be for kids.

In the nose of the trailer was a large, heavy crate. One of the guys shown a light on it. In bold black stencil it read: CONTENTS ONE (1) GUILLOTINE-ASSEMBLY REQUIRED-PROPERTY US GOVERNMENT FEMA.

"Guillotine? Like Mary Antoinette? What the fleeking hell?" Jake blurted out.

"That's what it says, damn," Brad said quietly. Sadie went to tell Bob.

Jake looked at Brad and Ken, "Why would FEMA need a guillotine packed in with all these coffins?" nobody answered, there was nothing to say.

Sadie came back, "Bob said to leave it on the truck. Can we cover it up with something? It gives me the creeps." Ken went to the hardware to get a tarp.

Wolfy had gone home to get some rest. He had gone around with Sam to check the barricades and the town one more time and was exhausted. His wife Marty heated up a can of soup for him and after he ate she made him lie down.

She was a quiet woman who understood the requirements of his job and supported him the best she could. She let him sleep but kept a watch just in case.

Bob got up to move Maggie around to the back of the store and backed it in the dock. He was wondering about what he had been hauling this past year.

He had delivered several times to underground facilities in Boyers, Pa. Denver, Kansas City and Helena, Montana. All the loads came from a warehouse in Oakland, California. He realized he really didn't want to think about it.

The Mayor with her secretary a pretty young woman named Tonya Spattson walked around town reassuring folks and checking on things in general.

They stopped at Millie's house. Miss Beachum answered the door dressed in an orange full length mumu decorated with big bright green smiley faces. On her head was a rhinestone tiara that said Happy New Year '63.

"Oh Mrs. Mayor, how delightful to see you, I was just thinking how what a good idea it would be that after all this commotion is over if I would donate that vacant lot I have behind the bank as a playground for the children. I'll even buy the equipment and pay to have it built." She said with a big smile.

Helen and Tonya were stunned. They had expected a diatribe of curses and threats. Helen put her hand to her breast and stammered, "Why Miss Millie that would be wonderful!"

Millie giggled like a school girl and said, "Yes, yes it would be." She turned and went back in her house.

Helen looked at Tonya who shrugged and said, "Go figure."

Colt Pride, a senior at South Forest High took up the post at the top of the lighthouse. With him was Corey Potts, Jarrod's little brother.

He had brought the 7.62 caliber German military rifle his dad had got him for his birthday. At the target range he put three holes in three shots in a fifty cent piece size circle at three hundred yards.

He raised the binoculars and scanned the area. He saw three canoes holding a group of men coming down the river.

"Corey," he said, "this doesn't look right."

That was when Clay, Sally and the other children said to Arnie who was splitting firewood, "Dad, Mr. Swende, there's trouble in Tionesta!"

# CHAPTER THIRTY SIX

B y this time the flu had ran its course. One week. Seven point two billion people were dead. Ninety eight percent of the worlds population.

The flu simply vanished. Viruses are like people, in order to live they destroy their means of survival.

However, this solved a lot of problems. There were no poor people anymore. If you needed something it was laying around. You simply went and found it.

No more unemployment. Everyone was now self-employed finding food. No housing problem. No taxes. No debt.

Cain would not slay Abel because there was nothing to get jealous about. No need for money, nothing was for sale. Diamonds were just pretty rocks once again.

The biggest problem a person had was avoiding all the dead bodies. The fires had burned themselves out. Pollution was over, no more global warming.

However, not all problems were solved. The astronauts on the space station were facing slow starvation. The scientists in Antarctica were doomed to freeze. In Russia a submarine docked and the crew was astounded by what they found.

The flu traveled far and fast but couldn't go everywhere. The Mashco Piro tribe of Peru were completely unaware of all these events until they began to listen to their children.

A small tribe deep in the Congo were unaffected, except that they couldn't understand the strange behavior of their offspring. Around the globe there were scattered individuals and groups the flu did not harm.

Many of those untouched were in northern Siberia, Greenland, Easter Island, many of the Pacific islands and other remote areas.

There were entire cities burnt to ruins, whole nations devoid of human life. Something unheard of was in the air, silence.

Somehow, by the merest flutter of a butterflies wings the town of Tionesta escaped the deadly scourge.

Of course only the children yet knew of these things. The Others began to seek out the survivors.

One last threat remained.

# CHAPTER THIRTY SEVEN

Rocky told them how it would go. His team would go down Little Hickory road, find canoes and silently approach from the river.

Jamal's group would come down German Hill to Sleepy Woman lane, follow that straight into the woods and emerge in the center of town and push to the main street. High fiving and tipping their bottles they departed on their separate ways.

Rocky's troop came to the highway and just like the old geezer said there was the canoe rental place. "Well," said Quince, "dey be renting cheap today."

There was a beer distributer there as well and they just couldn't help themselves. Shaking the cans and spraying themselves, laughing and carrying on they were on a roll.

In three boats the seven men set out. They laid the shotguns and rifles down on the floors to conceal them. They didn't care about the beautiful fall colors as the bright sunlight reflected the leaves off the river.

One of the bunch said they shoulda grabbed some fishing poles as well as the beer and fished as they floated down the Allegheny.

The other group didn't fare as well. Sleepy Woman lane turns off German Hill just before the Swende house comes into view. There were four camps on it and one resident at the very end, Sarey Spank.

Sarey was out back today with the blind beagle and the miniature white goat when the criminals approached her small trailer.

The dog began to growl, Frankie came around the side with his pistol and caught Sarey. The goat attacked him, butting him in the knees. Jamal shot the goat.

The men had Sarey in a circle. "Somebody shoot the bitch, we can't leave no one behind us." Jamal commanded.

"Wait man," said the feller sentenced to ten years for DUI, "let's have some fun first." He took a long pull on his bottle of Old Grandgag and ripped her blouse open. She screamed.

That's when three giant, fur covered creatures ran at them from the woods. The men were so shocked they never got their guns up before the beasts unleashed their terrible fury.

The man holding Sarey was swatted in the head, breaking his neck and crushing his skull. One grabbed Frankie and bit out half his throat then swung the body into two others knocking them to the ground.

The third grabbed the arm of the murderer next to Jamal, ripped it from his body and hit him with it.

The accountant shit himself when the first creature slapped the top of his bald head crushing the skull bone into his head.

Jamal tried to run but the largest of them grabbed him from behind, digging its fingers into his belly and ripping it apart. In seconds it was over.

One of the beasts picked up the limp, unmoving goat, held it to its bosom and emitted a thin wail. The largest walked up to Sarey blood dripping from its hands. Sarey cupped her hand to its cheek and powerful jaw and made a commiserate sound.

Corey, who was with Colt Pride sent his nonverbal message and his brother warned Ralph Lipton that men were coming down the river.

Ralph carried his rifle over to the riverbank just in time to see three canoes pull up to the beach landing. Jarrod joined Ralph.

"Howdy," said the man getting out of the middle of the first boat, "you know where we can get something to eat around here?"

"This town is under strict orders of quarantine. You can leave right now or stay in that tent over there for seventy two hours." Ralph told them sternly. Then his eyes strayed to the ungodly ugly hat the thin black man was wearing.

Rocky saw the distraction and grabbed his shotgun firing into Ralph then shot Jarrod as well. They all began to get out of the canoes and picking up their rifles. They weren't used to canoes and were having trouble getting out.

In town all the children screamed. The people working in the Superduper didn't hear the shots but Bob did. He got his defender model shotgun and climbed down off the truck. He started towards the front of the store but a great pain engulfed his chest. He first went to his knees and then on his face.

In the lighthouse Corey screamed and Colt who was watching through his scope took aim and fired. A bright pink hat rose in the air, he fired again.

Rocky heard the impact before the shot. Quince's head exploded, his stupid hat popped straight up in the air with part of his skull and brains still in it. Another bullet hit Lucas Leekus who fell at the landing. They took cover in front of the parked cars.

Penny Totters let out a scream and yelled that Jarrod was dead, stopping the workers in the store. They grabbed what guns they had and rushed out the front. They heard a shot from the lighthouse and Penny said, "Colt has them pinned down at the barricade."

Two more shots rang out in quick succession. Ken fired up the Jeep, in went Brad, Jake and Wade.

Rocky knew he had made a mistake by underestimating the situation. He should have watched the town for a day or two first. He took a drink from his gin bottle and thought, ah well spilt milk, boo hoo. He wondered where Jamal was. That would distract that damn sharpshooter.

Spang! Spang! Two more bullets hit the cars. He noticed that fifteen yards away was a bunch of pine trees that the sniper couldn't see through. "Okay guys, we're gonna run for those trees at his next shot." Rocky shouted out.

The jeep was coming around the bend to the barricade when Colt fired again, then two seconds later fired three quick shots emptying his clip.

The marauders reached the trees less one man shot on the run. Rocky saw the army Jeep coming and fired at it sixty feet away. The driver's head snapped back and it veered off the road and turned over, throwing the passengers clear.

Rocky made signs to two of the remaining men to go kill the men on the ground then stepped out from cover.

He felt like he had been punched twice in the chest. The gun fell from his hands, 'what's wrong?' were his final thoughts. From the side came more rifle fire getting the two killers approaching the men scattered on the ground.

The last criminal standing ran and dove in the river. He didn't last long as the current in the cold, deep water pulled him under.

Sheriff Wolfgang J Culpepper was awakened by his wife at the first shot. He grabbed his gun belt and his AR-15. He rode into battle on his wife's pink Schwinn. He arrived in time to gun down the fool who came out of the pine trees.

He then emptied his magazine at the two assassins who were headed for the wrecked Jeep. He ran down to the river bank but there was no sign of the last one, just a baseball hat floating in the water.

It was finished but the day wasn't over yet.

# CHAPTER THIRTY EIGHT

The children had remained on the ship at their own request that Addie hadn't felt good about. She trusted very few people.

She, Umberto and Professor Bond returned to the motel in San Luis Obispo. They found some food and ate a quiet, subdued dinner. There was a lot to think about.

Afterwards Gary took a flashlight and entered a book store. Umberto disappeared down the street. Addie changed out of the bikini into more practical clothes.

What they had learned that day was over whelming, it would take time to digest.

Gary returned with an armload of reading material. There were books on ancient Peru, the Mayans, (of course), the Assyrians and the pyramids.

"Gary," Addie asked, "they said they found no one else in the galaxy. Who or what were those serving creatures and how are their likenesses shown all over the place?"

"That's a very good question to start our next discussion with them." Gary mused, "Also did you notice they never once mentioned their names, why?"

"That's right! Gary you are very observant." Addie sighed, "More questions and more questions. Well, we'll have the rest of our lives to ask them. I am worried about the kids though." She had began to protest leaving the children there without her being there but then realized there was really nothing she could do about it. She prayed they would still be there when they returned the next day.

Gary left her for his own room and a little research. He paused to think. He, who had been educated at Berkley and Stamford thought how so much like autistic children we must seem to the Others. Our minds closed off, barely able to communicate.

The next morning Umberto was outside and had a large parrot with him that was cracking and eating walnuts. "I came outside and it flew down and came right up to me. I was eating a pear and it wanted some." He explained.

Addie was pleased to see the beautiful bird. Gary was not, having had a bad experience with a parrot in the past. He refrained from telling them about the bite sized piece of his buttocks that was missing.

They drove back to the cliff leaving the bird at the motel and the craft was still there. Addie sighed in relief.

Sasha and Ollie came out and brought them back in. Sasha said, "We meet 'ally and 'lay today." Gary patted her head and said, "That's nice." They didn't notice the opening to the outside disappearing behind them nor the ship ascending.

A different lady came to greet them, with the same white hair, white pajamas, and blue gem necklace at her breast. "I sense you are full of questions, please ask." The disembodied voice requested.

"The grey creatures . . ." Gary began.

"Ahh yes, our servants," she began, "we refer to them as intelligent plants. They were bioengineered from a most unusual plant resembling your Saguaro cactus from the area you call Arizona.

They were found on a world we were exploring. They have the most incredible ability to actually uproot themselves and walk in a fashion to a more suitable location.

They have no cognizant mind of their own except for basic instinct. We were able to cause them to grow thought centers and they can respond to simple commands. They can be taught complex tasks and retain their abilities in a form of memory.

You learned of them by accident, quite literally. One craft they were in to collect bio samples was struck by lightning and crashed in your New Mexico shortly after we returned to find you experimenting with nuclear fission once again.

Then the government of your nation was contacted by us through our servants to recover the wreckage. They released the images to get the general public familiar with them to ease disclosure which was inevitable. Sadly the catastrophe occurred just before this was to happen."

"Names," Addie asked, "do you have individual names?"

"We don't need them. We know who we are. None of us seek fame or fear that we will not be remembered. Each of us has a uniqueness that is singular. You call them souls.

The birth pangs of this new era of humanity are beginning to abate. Soon we will become healers such as we have never healed before. The study of your children has revealed to us the solution to the mystery that perplexed us all these millenniums.

The Earth originally had been exposed to a certain gamma ray caused by the combination of certain elements blasted by the superheat of the sun. One of those elements is so rare we had not been aware of its existence until just now. We call it rarium.

We believe that when the twin comets that destroyed our relatives so many eons ago somehow cloaked the effects of those rays. Therefore causing the defect, not only in your brains but in the brains of whales and porpoises as well. we are now able to communicate with them as well as your children.

We have developed a way to unblock your brains as well, giving you access to the total capacity of your minds.

But first we would like you to assist us in another contact." Sasha had crawled onto Gary's lap and was asleep. Ollie sat between Addie and Umberto and was resting his head on Addie's leg. The children were tired.

# CHAPTER THIRTY NINE

Bard came to and saw Sadie's face looking at him. She clutched his arm. "Oh good!" she exclaimed, "You've opened your eyes. Don't try to get up yet."

He remembered being in the Jeep but not what happened. He looked past Sadie and saw the vehicle lying on its side.

Mary was attending to Jake who had been riding in the passenger seat and had caught a couple pellets in his left arm. He had a mild concussion also.

Wolfy was looking at Ken who had been killed by the shotgun blast and Wade who's neck had been broken. By then several other townspeople had arrived at the scene.

Wolfy walked down by the river and was looking in the canoes when someone asked him what those men had been after.

"Judging from what's in these boats I'd say they wanted the beer distributor and the state store. Obviously those men were drunk."

That was when a shadow passed over them and looking up they all saw a huge boomerang shaped craft glide slowly over the town and disappear over German Hill.

Wolfy said to no one in particular, "This just ain't my day."

Brad was sitting up now and holding Sadie's hand when he asked her, "Where's Bob?"

Clay, Sally and the other kids all stopped what they were doing and looked at the adults sitting around the kitchen table. "We must all go outside now." They said in unison.

Arnie, Mattie, Becca and Sam who had joined them the night before walked out into the yard. Wolfy had thought it a good idea that

Sam take some time with his wife and he could help Arnie watch the road.

Sarey and her dog were walking up the driveway. Goofy ran with his tail wagging to greet them.

The massive ship came right over their heads and landed in the field out behind the barn. "The Others are here." Sally spoke for everyone.

Gary, Addie, Umberto and the children came out with three of the crew. Sally was delighted to see Sasha as she was tired of all the boys who greeted Ollie by tossing a ball at him which he deftly caught.

A small saucer shaped craft rose out of the mother ship and flew off back to town. The adults all greeted each other and started talking. Well, Gary started talking.

He was using such bombastic language that Sam yelled 'hey' at him and asked him to speak English. Gary had thought he was.

The saucer craft landed in the parking lot of the Superduper. Sadie didn't see it. She had found Bob laying on the asphalt the shotgun by his side.

She thought he was dead but felt a faint pulse in his neck. She started to cry and pray. She heard a voice in her head that asked, "May I help?"

She looked up and saw a young woman with white hair wearing white pajamas kneeling towards her. Sadie sat up straight, her hand still on Bob's back.

The woman removed a blue diamond drop shaped gem from around her neck and placed it on Bob's bare skin at the back of his neck. The gem glowed faintly and Bob coughed.

The lady retrieved her stone and stood up. Bob's eyes opened and he rolled over. He sat up looked at the two women and said with a sheepish grin, "I musta fell."

Sadie gasped and smiled, bringing her hands to her tear streaked face. "Oh thank God!"

Another white haired woman waited until Mary had removed Jake's shirt then touched her blue gemstone to his wounded arm. The pellets fell out and in seconds the skin had healed.

"Wow!" exclaimed Mary, "That thing would come in handy."

Wolfy walked up, still holding his rifle. He had it pointed at the ground. He said to the woman, "I see you mean us no harm."

The woman smiled and everybody heard in their heads, "No, no harm at all."

# CHAPTER FORTY

Seven days after the plane crash Grandfather woke George early. Without any breakfast he led him off deep into the canyon.

When it appeared they could go no further Grandfather stepped behind a boulder and disappeared. It was a hidden trail that led up.

They followed it, at one point they had to crawl along a narrow opening in the rocks. Then they came to a place where steps had been carved into the solid granite. "How did you . . . ?"

Grandfather shushed him with a violent hand swipe. "This is a sacred place," he whispered, "remain silent."

They climbed on a little way farther to a large open space. Grandfather began picking cactus fruit and cutting out the cores.

He led George over to an ancient fire ring where the black coals of some distant fire remained.

Taking a sprig of sage Grandfather shook it around a flat rock while intoning words in a low almost silent chant. He spread the fruit out on the rock to dry in the sun.

George was sent to quietly gather what firewood he could find and when he returned they sat facing each other.

No food, no water, no sounds, they sat motionless in the warm sunlight. When the evening shadows grew darker Grandfather took his obsidian knife and cut each fruit in half.

George lit a small fire. Grandfather shook the sage around the fire in a circle and then cast it into the flames. He gave George a half of each separate fruit and they ate them.

In the dim firelight George could see a bright aura surrounding his Grandfather who now began to speak.

"We are about to enter the eighth world now. In the beginning when Coyote, the trickster allowed us to emerge from the dark hole in the Earth he told of this time. The sky people will return at the end of this cycle. You, George Bluerock, have been chosen to lead the people into the future."

"But how can I lead anyone, I'm still a little kid?" George asked. He noticed his voice seemed to come from far away.

"You will not always be small. You will have the wisdom of the Gods," Grandfather intoned, "and I will be with you always to guide and help you."

Sparks from the fire wove intricate patterns in the dark and George watched them as they danced in the night.

He thought of the terrible scenes he had witnessed, not only with his own eyes but with the eyes of many. However, there were other sights also of children laughing, playing, an old man befuddled with feathers drifting around his head.

The sight of a vast forest with bright colored leaves surrounding him and one of a tower built on an island in a river.

He looked at the stars, endless in their beauty. They began to fade and he became frightened. It was merely the dawn, a new day was rising.

A large black object hovered overhead then moved to the east and landed. "Come," said Grandfather, "the future is here."

# CHAPTER FORTY ONE

Elmo was in the corral trying to get a loop over the stallion's head. All the horses were skitterish.

Pat was sitting on the top rail. Outside leaning on the same rail a slightly pregnant Sheila was laughing at Elmo. "Looks like he don't want ridden today." She jested.

They didn't know it but they were among the last of the survivers the Others had yet to contact. Sheila was about to become a very important lady by carrying the first child conceived after the gamma ray burst.

That's when Pat pointed out across the grassland, "Look at that!"

They saw the huge arc shaped craft come in and land a couple hundred feet away.

Elmo spat out a stream of tobacco juice and said, "See? I told you all them conspiracy nuts was right."

# CHAPTER FORTY TWO

Well, let's wrap it up now. Mattie finally told Arnie they were expecting. She had been approached by two white haired ladies who told her they were especially interested in the development of the fetus she was carrying.

Brad and Sadie became an item and soon a wee bit of work for Pastor Tom. Bob never drove Maggie again, she's still waiting behind the Superduper. Bob met Wade's widow and forgot about traveling the road. They did remove and destroy the guillotine though.

Colt Pride was celebrated as the hero of the battle for Tionesta. The last war ever fought on planet Earth.

The space station occupants were rescued along with the scientists in Antarctica. They found every living person stranded at sea.

The Others offered everyone their technology and the key to unlock their minds and join with them for the many long and exciting years to come. They explained to each and every survivor how the Earth, their home planet was special to them as the abundance of life was unique over all the other planets they had explored so far.

The fact that it could now be restored to its pristine condition and kept that way caused tears of joy in even the eldest among them.

The collective mind they now all shared was not an open book on each other's lives, although there was no reason why it shouldn't be. It was simply impolite to peek. Besides they could easily shield private thoughts or send a message seeking certain information.

The Others used computers far more advanced than anything we have ever imagined. Thoughts could control their machines and devices.

The jewels each of them wore were a sort of communication link which could manifest its signals into whatever form desired. They controlled the very atoms of substance. If a certain tool or food was desired their thoughts were made reality by the jewel, the magic of legend.

The effect of the jewels on the newest members had an interesting side effect as it reversed the aging process and everyone became a healthy young adult of the age of thirty. Those younger than that would age no longer when they reached that birthday.

With several more ship arriving from space the great clean up began. The waste and debris were disintegrated back to molecular form. The miles and uncounted tons of asphalt and concrete turned back into rich fertile soil.

The garbage and abandoned, sunken ships of the oceans removed and recycled. The combustible engine was obsolete, no reason to use the deadly poison oil ever again.

All radioactive material was obliterated. The rivers were undammed and allowed to follow their natural courses. Soon the streams and rivers were running clear and the water was drinkable. The filth of mankind was erased.

Wildlife returned in abundance to the forests and fields. Birds filled the skies and the oceans teemed with fish. The Earth was given over to caretakers like George Bluerock and his wise Grandfather.

The Others had harnessed the free and non-toxic energy of the Universe. There was an unlimited amount.

The planet became a sparkling blue jewel once again to be preserved forever.

There was a ceremony joined by all the humans across the galaxy to celebrate the end of Homo Sapiens and the beginning of Homo Conjunctus.

They were ready to explore the depths of the Universe.


The end of the beginning.

I wish to thank all the very nice ladies at the Sarah Stewart Bovard Memorial Library in Tionesta for their gracious help and support in making this dream come true. Also my dear Mary who's love, support, and constructive criticism helped in uncountable ways.

Please believe me when I say this book is a work of fiction. All characters mentioned are products of my imagination and if they resemble anyone in real life then it is just a coincidence.

The town of Tionesta is real however. It does indeed have a lighthouse and breathtaking scenery. I hope you enjoyed this, thank you for reading. Bob.